TWO COWBOYS' CHRISTMAS BRIDE

LACEY DAVIS

VIRTUAL BOOKSELLER

❀ Created with Vellum

An Unexpected Christmas Present

After her uncle sells her to a brothel, Anna Best is
kidnapped. Terrified and tied up inside a tow sack, she's
dumped on the doorstep of two Texas Rangers.

Mack and Jake think Santa has come early when they
unwrap the package to discover a beautiful brunette with a
feisty spirit.

One look convinces them she will be theirs, that they will
protect her from a crazy uncle determined to enslave her.
Only a wedding ring, their badges, and six shooters can
keep her safe right where she belongs—in their arms and
their bed.

With Mack and Jake, will Anna have the family she craves
or will her greedy family destroy her happiness?

Sign up for my New Book Alert and receive a free book — Blindfold Me.

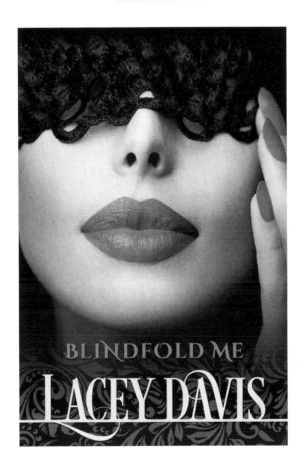

https://www.subscribepage.com/laceydavis_author

CHAPTER 1

*A*nna Best never dreamed her life could go so wrong. Two weeks before Christmas, her uncle sold her to the local whorehouse. One evening before the madam of the house could sell off her virginity, she'd been drugged and abducted.

Now she found herself in a rough tow sack that smelled like potatoes being hauled around in the back of a wagon. Whoever opened this bag better be prepared, because she would come out fighting.

Anna was no simpering woman and she was aching to give a good tongue lashing. The bouncing of the wagon had jolted her awake to her head pounding, her wrists tied, her mouth covered, and stuffed in a bag.

Not exactly how she'd planned her escape from the brothel.

The wagon wheels came to a stop and she listened as two voices whispered in the darkness.

"Is this the right place," a female voice said.

"I think so," a young man replied.

"Come on, lift her out of the wagon and let's leave her on the doorstep."

Anna wanted to scream, but all she could do was make muted noises. Still, she could kick.

"Good thing you stuffed her mouth, Ma."

Ma? A woman was involved in her kidnapping?

Fury roared through her as they dragged the gunnysack along the back of the wagon. She kicked and flailed her legs trying to create as much havoc for them as possible.

"Stop moving, girl, or I will drop you right here in the dirt," the woman said quietly.

Where did she know that voice from?

Tiring, she stopped thrashing as they carried her then set her down on the cold ground.

"Let's go," the woman whispered in the darkness.

"Won't she freeze to death?" a young male voice asked.

"Not this one. The devil is strong within her," the woman said.

What? Did the woman believe she wanted to be taken to a whorehouse? To have her uncle, a family member, sell her? All she had asked for in life was a loving family. And look where that had gotten her.

Sold to a brothel.

As they walked away, the sounds of their retreating footsteps crunching on the ground sent fear slamming into Anna. Trembling, she lay balled up in the darkness, unable to discern where they left her. What if wild wolves or coyotes found her?

What if she died right here inside this bag?

The cold started to creep into the potato sack. In Blessing, Texas, the winters were mild, but still she started to shake. It was December, not exactly a hot summer day.

Doubled over inside the bag, she didn't have room to stretch her legs and they were going numb. She rolled and came up against a hard surface. A barn? House?

Rocking inside the bag, she hit the wall.

Bang!

Did anyone live here? Did she want to find out?

Bang.

Bang.

Tiring, her shoulder throbbing, she heard a noise.

A door opened.

"What the hell?"

"Hold that lantern a little higher, Mack," a voice said.

"What's the note say?" a deeper male voice asked.

"Merry Christmas."

Anna's temper exploded. She writhed and screamed as much as she could inside the bag.

The men cursed. "Someone's in there."

With relief, she felt them untying the bag and pulling it down then lifting her to her numb feet. Her eyes were blinded by the light of the lantern.

"Oh my God, it's a woman."

"A damn fine-looking woman," the other man said.

Slowly her eyes adjusted to the light as she stared at two extremely handsome men standing in the doorway without shirts on. Muscled arms and chests with wisps of dark hair glowed in the warm light.

Who were these men and why had she been delivered here?

"Santa brought us an early Christmas present. A

woman."

CHAPTER 2

*J*ake stared at the brunette, her ice-blue eyes flashing with anger, her fists raised ready to fight in a dress only a whore would wear. White lace and silk barely covered her breasts, though they were spilling out of the low-cut top. Her pebbled nipples shining through the material.

The skirt was above her knees and she wore white hosiery that stopped near her thighs, though her legs were long and shapely.

If he believed her outfit, she was a high-class whore, but what if she were kidnapped like his sister? And why had she been dumped on their doorstep?

"I don't know what happened to you tonight, but I get the feeling you're in trouble," Jake said softly trying to calm her.

"I'm not going to be any man's whore," she said with a spat, her beautiful full mouth curled in a snarl.

The feisty woman looked delectable. Good enough to eat from head to toe, but anger sizzled from her and she looked like she was prepared to punch anyone who came near her.

"I'm Jake Nash and this is my partner, Mack Savage. We're Texas Rangers."

"Really, you're Texas Rangers?" she asked. "How do I know for certain?"

"You can take a look at our badges," Jake told her.

A frown furrowed her brow and she shook her head. "Why was I delivered to your doorstep?"

"Lady, that's what we'd like to know," Mack said. "From the way you're dressed, I don't think you were attending the church social tonight."

A smile spread across her lips and yet Jake could still see the wariness in her stance. Like she was prepared for battle.

"How did you get in that tow sack?"

"I don't know," she said. "Are you part of the plan? Someone must have planned to drop me off here."

Jake shook his head. She was being very cautious and yet he couldn't blame her. "We're not part of any plan. Mack, grab our badges and bring her a shirt."

It had been a long time since he'd experienced a woman and this one had all the right curves in all the right places. If he had to stare at her near nakedness much longer, he'd be shedding his clothes and sinking his cock deep within her.

Already he was hard with lust. If he had to stare at her rosy nipples and long legs that ended in a cunny that he was certain wasn't covered, he'd be breaking his oath to never force himself on a woman. Because this one was a temping morsel.

Mack handed her a shirt to cover herself. She slid her arms in the sleeves and wrapped the material around her. The hem hung just below her cunny.

She stared at the badges and nodded. "Thank God."

"Now, tell us how you got in that tow sack. Tell us what happened to you," Mack said as he gazed at her.

With a sigh, he took her arm and she let him lead her to their couch where she sank down. "My uncle sold me to the brothel. Mrs. Leake's place. Tonight was the night they were going to auction me. After they dressed me, I stood waiting in the kitchen, hoping for a chance to escape, when suddenly a rag covered my nose and I passed out. When I awoke, I was bouncing around in the back of a wagon inside a potato sack. When we stopped, I fought my kidnappers. The woman told me to stop or she would drop me. A young man called her *ma*. A woman kidnapped me. A mother. They left me in the dark, sitting on the ground, in the cold until you opened the door."

Jake glanced at Mack and he could see his confusion. Why would someone bring the woman here?

"You didn't order me?"

"No," Mack said. "We like our women willing. It's against our honor to do something to a woman against her will."

The room was chilled and Mack stoked the fireplace, causing the embers to come to life as flames sparked.

Her face seemed to relax and her hands stopped shaking.

Jake shook his head, puzzled. "Do you think they brought you here because they thought you would be safe?"

The woman's big blue eyes were framed by long, dark lashes. Her cheekbones were high and she had a narrow short nose that had a cute lift at the end. But her mouth was mesmerizing with her full lips that begged to be kissed.

Long hair curled down past her shoulders to her hips. And Jake imagined pulling her hair to bring her mouth to his cock that was like granite.

"How would I know? I never saw them. I never knew anything until I woke up in the back of their wagon."

Jake observed the woman. Was this a trick? Could she be lying to them? "What's your name?"

"Anna Best."

"Nice to meet you, Anna," Mack said.

Already Jake could see that Mack was enamored with the woman, but Jake was a little more cautious. Were they being set up?

"Your uncle sold you," Mack asked as he turned to Jake.

Anger roiled inside of Jake, all the pain and fury rising from the depths of him. All the hurt of the memory of his sister. His first instinct was to kill her uncle. No one should ever be sold into prostitution.

Jake knew his facial expression had changed because she glared back at him. "Why would your uncle sell you?"

The woman frowned. "When I was sixteen, my parents were murdered. No one has found their killers. Since then, my uncle has been taking care of me." She sighed and shook her head. "You might say I have not been the easiest person to live with."

If you loved someone you didn't sell them into slavery. No matter what they did. There was something more, but she was protecting him. Why, he had no idea. The man deserved to be strung up.

"Who is your uncle?"

She bit her bottom lip and Jake almost groaned. His cock was straining just knowing what she wore under that shirt. Her full breasts, the glimpse of her long legs when they lifted her from the bag. He'd take her right now, if he could. But that was impossible. She had suffered enough trauma for one night.

"I'm not saying," she said.

There it was, her protecting him once again. Why?

"I'd like the chance to get even," she said softly, but her eyes reflected an eagerness that showed she wanted to make this man suffer.

She wanted vengeance.

"How?" Mack asked. "You're a woman."

She gave him a searing look that should have singed his dark hair. The woman had spirit and he liked that about her.

"I know how to get to him," she said. "Better than anyone. I know all his secrets."

Outside, an owl hooted. It was fewer than two weeks until Christmas and here they were sitting inside the house with a near naked woman. A house they rented while they were in town. Not a real home, but just a place to lay their heads at night.

"You haven't decorated for Christmas," she said frowning. "It's next week and you don't have a tree."

It was clear that she was distracting them from talking about her uncle. And that made Jake all the more curious.

"Can I spend the night?" she said. "I'm not going to face

my uncle wearing these clothes and well, I need some time to hide out. I'm sure Mrs. Leake is searching for me."

Oh, yes, she would have her henchmen combing the streets, looking for her new girl.

"Are you a virgin?" Jake asked. He knew it was inappropriate, but he also knew how these brothels worked. Auctioning off her virginity would bring the owner a lot of money. If Mrs. Leake knew she had a virgin, she'd be salivating to get her hands back on her.

The woman stood and put her hands on her hips. Her blue eyes sparkled in the light of the fireplace. "Of course, I am."

"Then yes, she's going to be searching for you, hoping to find you before someone breaks your maidenhead, losing her a lot of money," Jake replied.

Yes, his words were cruel, but true. He'd seen how this worked when they stole his sister. And he was determined to put these ruthless operations out of business. This one had just been placed on his list to stop the owner's detestable treatment of women.

A blush spread across her face. "All I want is a chance to get revenge on my uncle. Then I don't care what happens."

Mack stood and went to her side. "You stay here for a few days. Hide out and we'll help you."

The woman tilted her head and licked her lips as she stared at Mack. "I'm safe?"

Jake wanted to laugh but didn't.

"Honey, with a body like that, you're not safe anywhere," Jake told her. "My cock is so hard, it's about to burst. But we're honorable men. We would never take advantage of you."

It was true. As much as he wanted to fuck her right now, he would never ruin a virtuous woman until she asked him to. And right now, he was praying she would beg them to take her. But what she didn't realize was that they shared everything.

They were partners. What one had, so did the other. And it would take a special woman to accept that when they married, she would have not one, but two men protecting her.

Already he could hear her sweet voice crying out in pleasure. Picture her splayed naked across the bed while he plunged his hard cock into her tight, willing cunny.

"It's time for you to go to bed," Mack said, and Jake knew he was feeling the same way.

"Your bedroom is down the hall there. Our bedrooms are upstairs."

She started to take Mack's shirt off.

"Oh no, wear the shirt. We'll find you some clothes tomorrow."

"Thank you," she said and glanced at each of them and smiled. "You men make me feel safe for the first time in days."

If only she knew what he was thinking, she wouldn't feel safe any longer. Because he wanted to slip his fingers into her sweet cunny and taste her passion. He wanted to hear her screaming with pleasure. He wanted to make her come all over his cock.

CHAPTER 3

*M*ack had barely slept the rest of the night. His bed felt empty and lonely and his mind kept traveling back to the gorgeous scantily clad woman downstairs. She seemed innocent and yet she also was ready to take the two of them on. A feisty female determined to go down fighting.

Every time she moved, that dress would reveal a new part of her skin that had his cock rigid. All that silky flesh exposed that he wanted to explore. That he wanted to sink his cock into.

This morning, they had left her alone in the house and ridden out hoping to catch the masked bandit robbing the stage. The next one was due to arrive later today. They spent the day hiding along the trail, waiting. But the robber did not appear.

They followed the horse-drawn rattletrap into town. As soon as the man riding shotgun blew the stage horn, they rode in closer. As the reinsman pulled into the station in

Blessing, Texas, Mack and Jakerode their horses to him as he descended from the box.

"Mack Savage, Texas Ranger and this is my partner Jake Nash. We're investigating the robberies you've experienced lately."

The driver shook his head as he gazed at their badges. "The son of a bitch seems to know whenever we're carrying gold. That's the only time we have any trouble."

How could the man know when they were expecting a shipment of gold?

"Isn't that information kept confidential?"

"Supposed to be," the man said, continuing to unload suitcases. "Don't know who is leaking the information, but we've been robbed recently three times."

Jake walked around the stagecoach. "Where do you hide the gold?"

"Normally, it's in a suitcase or trunk on the back. Lately, we're putting the box up in the front between the drivers. Wish you guys would catch this asshole. I'm not willing to die to keep the bank's shipment of gold safe."

Mack nodded his head. "Understand."

The driver unloaded the last of the trunks. "I've already put in for a different route."

"So you think that someone is telling the masked bandit when there is a shipment of gold?"

The man nodded. "Yes, I do. He's learning the information from somewhere."

A wagon filled with goods rolled down Main Street and Mack moved his horse closer to the sidewalk. "Who would know about the shipment?"

"Myself, the banker, the stage line and obviously the masked bandit."

"Do you keep the gold in the boot?"

"Yes, the one under the driver's seat, but he knows where it's at. Always tells us to remove the gold from the boot. So he knows it's there."

That really wasn't a big revelation. Most people knew they kept the gold in the boot.

"Were you the reinsman when the man riding shotgun was killed a couple of weeks ago?"

The man sighed. "If you're talking about Gerard Jones's death, yes. The man refused to give up the gold until he was shot. By the time we reached Blessing, he was dead."

They nodded.

"Thanks for the information. If we need anything else, we'll be in touch with you," Mack said and pulled his reins, leading his horse away.

For a moment, neither one of them said anything as they rode away. They noticed a group of men standing around a poster outside Leake's House of Pleasure, the local whorehouse.

Anna.

It said she had run away and they were searching for her.

"That's Josephine's new girl," an older man said. "There was supposed to be an auction last night to see who would pay the highest amount to claim her virginity."

"I'd fuck her," another man said.

Anger gripped Mack's chest and he pulled his horse away leading him down the road. He couldn't sit there and listen to the men talk about Anna that way. He just couldn't without his fists getting involved and that would only arouse suspicion.

"Looks like she was telling us the truth," Jake said, riding alongside him.

"Could you believe that dress she was wearing last night," Mack said.

"What dress? It was a few scraps of material that were placed in strategic locations. We need to stop at the mercantile. She can't continue to parade around the house in that outfit unless you want me taking her right there on the kitchen table."

Mack laughed. "Agree. Last night I couldn't sleep. All I could think about was putting my cock in her sweet cunny."

A loaded down wagon passed them on the street, the driver calling out to his mules.

"I know. But she's been betrayed and we're going to need to give her some time to learn to trust us."

It sounded like Jake had already claimed her as theirs. And Mack knew he would love nothing more than for the two of them to make her theirs with or without a wedding ring, but preferably with one.

Mack nodded, but his cock was twitching with eagerness to explore her flesh. And yet, he wasn't even sure she would be there when they got home. For all he knew, she could be gone.

"Let's stop and get her some clothes," Jake said. "I can't take another night of her in that piece of nothing."

"What if they ask us about buying women's clothes?"

"We tell them my sister is coming to visit," Jake said.

15

Mack knew the story of Jake's sister and she would never visit.

"A dress, but no pantaloons," Mack said. Just the idea that she would be naked beneath her dress, left his cock pulsating.

Her being there waiting for them was not good, and yet, Mack felt more excited about returning home than he could remember.

"What do we say when she asks us about pantaloons?" Jake asked.

Mack grinned, thinking of how he would spend days thinking about lifting her skirts and plunging into her sweet, wet pussy.

"We pretend we didn't know she needed them. But we'll know she's naked under that dress."

"Oh, God, how you like to torture me. I'll be a walking hard on."

Stepping out of his saddle, his feet hit the ground. "You wouldn't be buying pantaloons for your sister."

Jake laughed. "Not if I wanted to live. A small pint, she could fight better than a man."

They stepped onto the wooden sidewalk, their boots echoing.

"Come on, let's get this dress and get home. I'm anxious to see her in that outfit again. That wispy piece of lace didn't even hide her nipples," Mack said, thinking of how he wanted to peel that dress from her body, real slow and explore under every inch as the material fell to the floor.

"Yes, it was all I could do not to get up and taste one," Jake said, walking into the mercantile.

"That would have gotten you punched. She was ready to fight last night."

"That she was. And though she would have lost and I would have enjoyed the fight, I want her to trust us and approve of us. Because I'm thinking I might want to be her man."

There it was. Jake wanted them to claim her, and Mack knew it was only a matter of time.

Mack smiled. "You may be right."

CHAPTER 4

*H*er rangers had been gone all day. While they were out, she'd tidied up their place and rummaged through their closets until she found a fresh shirt and pair of pants she could wear. The brothel outfit had been so risqué and sexy and made her feel beautiful, but that wasn't her.

And the outfit was much too revealing. It was the kind of dress a woman only wore for her husband, and she didn't have a man.

Unless they forced her to return. She would never become a prostitute. Never. Not even for her uncle.

This afternoon, she had found a roast in the root cellar and she put some potatoes and carrots with the meat and baked it in the oven. It had taken her forever to get a good fire going in the oven, but now she had the food cooking. It was the least she could do for the men who were letting her stay with them. The table was set and she even made a buttermilk pie.

Suddenly the door opened and she jumped from setting

the table. She picked up a pan and was prepared to fight when Mack entered the kitchen.

"Darling, I don't know what's cooking, but it smells damn good," he said.

A smile spread across her face and her heart beat a little faster. If she were married, would this be the way her husband would come home and greet her? The only thing better would be if he kissed her, and gazing at his full lips, she wondered how he would taste.

With a sigh, she put the pan down. "Sorry, I didn't know when to expect you and was afraid someone unwelcome was entering the house."

He grinned.

Jake strolled in and glanced at her. "I was really hoping you were wearing that saloon dress again."

A trickle of something hot spiraled down her spine and centered in her middle. "Sorry, I rummaged around in your closets and found these pants and shirt. I hope you don't mind."

"Oh, I mind. Not nearly as pretty," Jake said, his eyes raking her body, causing a stir of warmth through her.

The memory of him saying she would never be safe came to mind and her breath became raspy.

"Or revealing," Mack said, a naughty grin on his face.

The men were making her feel uncomfortable the way they were gazing at her. Like she was dessert, and yet, she trusted them. For some reason, after last night, she was certain they would never harm her. Yet her body was responding to their heated glances.

When she gazed into Mack's emerald eyes, she liked the way they twinkled in a friendly kind of way, but when she looked in Jake's dark brown eyes, a rush of something warm heated in her center. It was like the man's gaze told her to remove any clothing between them. She wanted to feel his naked skin against her own.

Never before had she ever experienced such a feeling. Such warmth centered in her womanly regions. An unanswered need.

"Homemade cooking," Jake said.

Mack grinned. "Is that a pie sitting over there?"

"Yes," she said with a smile, glad the atmosphere suddenly felt less charged.

"Oh my, we've died and gone to heaven," Mack said. "I could get use to this."

Jake held out a wrapped package. "We got you this."

A smile spread across her face. She took the package and ripped it open. Inside was a red dress with a white undershirt. A modest dress she could wear in public and around the house. One that didn't make her appear to be a wanton.

She pulled the dress out of the wrapper. There were no pantaloons, chemise, corset or even a shift. It was only a dress. But then again, they were men. What did they know about what a lady wore under her clothing?

"Oh, thank you," she said. "Now I can go out in public again."

"No, you can't," Mack said. "Mrs. Leake has wanted posters of you around town. She's even offering a reward."

Anna felt her heart sink inside her chest. "Bitch."

Mack started laughing.

No, it was not a word a lady used, but then again, she

wanted to turn her from being a lady into being a whore. Anna would resist until she took her last breath.

"That she is," Jake agreed.

"You need to stay here until we catch our outlaw. Then we can discuss what you should do," Mack said.

They were searching for an outlaw in Blessing? Who? A trickle of alarm scurried down her spine. There was an outlaw in her family. A man she knew she could send to the gallows or even to prison. One that she used to respect, but not anymore.

Holding the dress up to her, she gazed at the two men, her heart pounding in her chest. What was it about these two handsome men that caused her blood to heat and her breathing to increase? Just looking at them had fire racing through her veins.

Never before had this happened to her. Never had she been so attracted to two men. Not one, but two. How in the world could she decide between them? But then again, maybe they weren't drawn to her like she was to them.

"Someone is robbing the stage. We're here to catch them," Mack said.

Her heart skipped a beat. She knew the person robbing the stage. She knew where the boxes of gold were hidden. It was the reason she was sold to the brothel, her life threatened.

"About three weeks ago, the Shotgun was killed in a stage robbery," Jake said. His eyes were gazing at her like he could read her mind.

"What's the Shotgun?"

"He's the man who guards the stage. He lost his life

when the robber shot him when he refused to give up the gold."

Finally, her uncle's misdeeds were going to catch up with him. He'd killed a man. Since her parents' death, she'd known he was dangerous. Even suspected him in the death of her mother and father. But when sixteen with no place to go, you laid low until old enough to leave. To find someplace to go...until you get caught.

And now it seemed that she was learning that Uncle Walter most definitely could kill someone. Did he murder her parents?

"I may know who you're looking for," she said, gazing at the two men, who now turned their attention on her. A heat began to rise in her body at the way they stared at her, their eyes peeling the shirt and pants from her body.

Maybe when this was over, she could have one of them, but right now, she wanted them both.

"Who?" Mack asked.

Knowing that they would not want her to be involved, she gazed at them and wondered if they would agree. "If I tell you, I get to participate in catching him."

"No," Jake said immediately. "It's too dangerous."

"Why would you want to?" Mack asked.

This was what attracted her to these men. One was so protective and the other listened to reason. He wanted to understand before he said no. They were like having one really good, solid man.

Picking up the pot pads, she reached in the oven to lift out the roast. This gave her a moment or two to consider her words carefully.

"It's your uncle," Jake said.

She almost dropped the roast. But still he didn't know the name of the man who had been her guardian for the last two years. Who she suspected had murdered her parents to take the ranch from her. Who sold her to a brothel to live a life on her back.

Carefully, she set the roast on the table, stood, and gazed at her two rangers. "Will you let me get the satisfaction of seeing him caught and captured?"

"No," Jake said.

"Yes," Mack replied.

They turned and glanced at one another. Finally, Jake gave a growl. "All right. But you will have to follow my instructions and not get in the way."

She grinned. "Oh, I'll follow your instructions, but I can't promise not to get in the way. You see Walter Farris is my uncle. The reason he took me to the whore house is because I found the gold. He caught me in his vault looking for evidence if he killed my parents. But I found so much more."

CHAPTER 5

*M*ack knew immediately what they must do. And he was certain that Jake would agree with him, but first they needed to talk. Alone.

After all, he knew that Jake was attracted to Anna, but would he marry her? And good Lord, after seeing her in that dress from the brothel, Mack was ready to say *I do* and sink his cock deep in her pussy.

Last night, he'd lay in his bed, yanking off like a teenage boy dreaming of peeling that dress from her body and exploring every inch. All day, he'd thought about this woman, feeling certain she was the one.

He grabbed Jake by the arm. "Excuse us a moment."

Anna gazed at him, those big blue eyes filled with surprise as he hauled Jake out of the kitchen.

"We need to talk," he told his friend as he dragged him through the front door. "Are you thinking what I'm thinking?"

"Depends," Jake said. "All night I dreamed of fucking her. But she needs our protection. Mrs. Leake is going to find her and then they will do everything they can to get her back to that whorehouse."

It was all Mack could do not to laugh. He'd been in the same predicament. After seeing all that exposed flesh last night, he wanted to run his finger over her skin, touch the silkiness between her legs.

A cold wind blew and the leafless trees branches swayed. Mack liked the little town of Blessing, but did he like it enough to live here forever?

"Maybe I was right last night," Mack said with a grin. "Maybe Santa really did bring us a gift. We've talked about finding a woman, marrying her and sharing her. Anna needs our help."

Jake, the more practical of the two, carefully considered his words. "This is forever."

"Yes, it is," Mack said. "And she would probably want to stay here in this little town."

Jake rubbed his hand over his face. "Since she landed on our doorstep, I've had this insistent urge to protect her. Keep her safe. And if her uncle is our criminal, then she doesn't even know how much danger she's in."

A man on horseback rode by and gazed at the two of them standing outside the house talking.

"Eventually, they're going to realize we have her," Mack said. "Eventually someone is going to come after her."

Jake noticed another man down the street watching them. Seemed like a lot of activity on their residential block. Could the word have gotten out about them buying a woman's dress and everyone suspected it to be Anna?

"We're being watched," Jake told his friend. "Seems the mercantile owner might be wanting to collect that reward."

"Damn," Mack said glancing around. "In the twenty-four hours we've known her, she has a feisty spirit that instantly drew me."

And a body that he ached to touch. There was something about Anna that had him knowing she was the one for him and Jake. There wasn't a question in his mind that she was their woman.

"So do you want to marry her?"

"Yes, I do," Mack said. "That would give her some protection."

"Agreed," Jake said. "But it's forever."

"Absolutely," Mack said with a grin. "If she'll agree to our terms, I think we just got ourselves a wife."

Jake smiled, which was a seldom thing. "Let's go talk to her."

Mack opened the door and the two of them entered the house. She had gone into her room and when she came out, she was wearing the new dress they bought her. As she walked into the living room, they stared at the woman Mack soon hoped to propose to.

The dress fit her to perfection, showing off curves in a more modest way. Mack would be proud to call her his wife.

"Darling, that dress looks good on you," Jake said, beating Mack to complimenting her.

"Thank you, this is more like what I'm accustomed to wearing."

All Mack could think about was that she couldn't be wearing anything under it. Because they deliberately didn't buy her undergarments. And now she would no longer need them, if she agreed to their proposal.

"You look beautiful," Mack finally said, nervous she wouldn't agree to the proposal.

"Let's eat," she said enthusiastically. "I'm starving and we don't want the food getting cold."

"Wait," Mack said. "First there's something we need to talk about."

"While we were outside, there were two men hanging about. Though we told the people in the mercantile we were buying this dress for my sister, I think they contacted Mrs. Leake. Sooner or later they're going to realize you're here," Jake said, stepping toward her.

Her sky-blue eyes widened and she clasped her hands in front of her. "I'm not going back to the brothel."

"No, you're not," Mack said, stepping close to her. "The only way to keep them from taking you is to marry you. Make you ours."

Her head jerked toward Mack and her brows drew together in a frown. "Marry you? Ours?"

Jake took her hand, his voice deep, his brown eyes dark with passion. "Mack and I share everything. One of us would marry you, but you would be a wife to both of us. We would share you in the bedroom and out."

He watched as her mouth dropped open. "How is that possible?"

Mack took her other hand. "We would share both your pussy and your ass. Eventually we would take you together."

Jake moved closer to her and Mack moved around to her back.

"We would honor and cherish you and create a family with you. You will want for nothing and each night we will make you scream with pleasure," Mack said, moving in close behind her, pressing his cock into her buttocks.

Jake stepped in to sandwich her between them. "Most of all, you'd be protected. Safe. Cherished and well loved."

"But I can't marry you both," she said, her voice whispery soft.

"No, one of us will be your legal husband, but the other one will be your husband as well."

She licked her lips nervously and then Mack watched as Jake took her in his arms, his mouth came down and claimed hers. His lips moving over hers as he kissed her, deeply and thoroughly.

Jake released her and Mack twirled her around to face him.

His mouth came down on her sweet lips as he pressed into her, letting her feel his stone hard cock as his lips ravished her mouth. Moaning deeply in her throat, he released her and Jake twirled her to face him.

"As your husbands, we will expect you to obey us or you will be punished."

"What? How?" she asked breathlessly.

"We will turn you over our knee and give your beautiful ass a spanking," Mack said as he gripped her full buttocks. The woman had a nice firm ass and he couldn't wait to lay a hand on it.

Her face was flushed and her lips swollen, and her breath was coming in short little rasps. The woman was obviously a virgin as she stood there in shock staring at Jake.

"Do you agree?"

Mack watched the tumultuous emotions cross the

beautiful woman's face. He could see she wasn't certain about the idea of them controlling and spanking her.

"Yes," she finally said as she gazed at the two of them. "As long as you don't hurt me."

"We would never harm you, but you might feel a little pain," Jake said. "If something happens to one of us, you'll always have the other one to protect you and make certain you're well cared for."

A tense silence filled the room as they stared at the beautiful woman that Mack was so ready to fuck.

"Anna, will you marry us?" Mack went down on one knee, asking the question he was unable to hold back any longer. Jake joined him and took her hand in his as they both gazed up at her.

For a moment, he feared she would say no as she gazed in shock at both of them. Then a timid smile crossed her face.

"Yes," she said. "But you'll need to be patient with me. Two men at once."

They both rose from bended knee and squeezed her between them with Mack's cock pressed into her round backside and Jake's into her pussy.

A gasp sounded from her. "When are we getting married?"

"The sooner the better," Mack said. "My cock has been rock hard since you arrived last night."

Jake reached down and placed his mouth over her breasts. With envy, Mack watched as she laid her head back against his shoulder. "Oh."

"Tonight. As soon as we eat," Jake said rising. "Until then, there will be no sex between us. So we better hurry."

Mack let his hand slide up her thigh under her dress until he reached her ass, which was naked. His fingers glided over her full cheeks and he couldn't wait to fuck her. Anna leaned into him and moaned.

Damn, she liked the feel of his hand on her ass.

"Let's eat and then let's go. Tonight we make you ours."

CHAPTER 6

*J*ake pulled the wagon to the back of the house. Too many eyes were watching in the front and he didn't want a fight until after the ceremony. When he was certain no one was looking, Mack quickly put Anna in the back of the wagon and covered her with a tarp.

"I'm getting really tired of this," she said. "This is the last time."

He chuckled. Their soon-to-be wife was a spitfire and he couldn't wait to tame her. Or maybe she would tame them, but either way, tonight would be their wedding night.

Mack climbed in the wagon. "Let's go."

It was still early enough that the sun had yet to set. They would arrive at the church just before dark.

Jake clicked to the horses and the wagon pulled away and turned onto the residential street where they were staying.

"Who's marrying her?" Jake asked his friend. No matter

what, he trusted Mack and knew they would share Anna. Just like he would always share with his friend.

Mack reached in his pocket and pulled out a coin. "Heads, I'm the legal husband, tails you're the one saying I do."

While the wagon rolled, he tossed the coin into the air and caught it in in his hand. When he opened his palm, he smiled. "Looks like she'll be Mrs. Jake Nash."

Jake nodded. He was fine with that, though he felt certain his wife would not take to being under his control quite as much as he wanted. The idea of her going after her uncle sent fear spiraling through him as the memory of his sister came to mind.

Because of Laura, he had become a Texas Ranger. Because of her abduction, he could not abide the mistreatment of women. Any woman.

Though he had a strong personality and would not accept disobedience, he would never harm or hurt a woman. Though he would paddle her ass if she disobeyed. And would protect his soon-to-be wife with his life.

"Let's get her to church," he said.

They were being followed.

"We've got company," he said, glancing back at the gunman on a horse following them.

Mack pulled out his gun and made certain the chamber had a bullet. "A new version of shotgun wedding."

Jake laughed. "Never thought of it that way, but I guess you could call it that."

The rider following at a discreet distance, suddenly turned down a side street as they pulled up in front of the church. "He's gone for help."

"Let's get her inside and get this done. There's going to be trouble."

Jake set the brake and then tied the reins of the horses while Mack jumped out of the wagon. He threw back the tarp and helped Anna out.

"Don't ever ask me to do that again," she said, her eyes wild looking. "I'm not afraid."

"Well, you should be," Jake said. "We were followed and now I think he's gone to get help."

Taking her by the arm, with the two of them on either side of her, they led her into the church.

A small chapel filled with benches and a large wooden cross at the front. They stared at the beauty of the place as they waited. Jake could remember his mother insisting they all attend service every Sunday morning. He would want the same for his own children.

A man came from the back. "Can I help you?"

"Yes, we want to get married. Right away."

"All right, let me just grab my Bible."

"Make it quick, preacher. Trouble is headed this way," Mack told him.

The man's eyes widened as he gazed at Anna. "You're the woman they're searching for."

"Yes," she said. "And if you don't hurry, I'm going to be forced to return."

The man ran to the back and when he returned, he began to say the vows.

Jake stared at the woman he was committing his life to. The woman he would protect. No, he didn't love her, but he could see himself falling for her. He could see the three of them raising a family together. Of babies being born and little ones running through the house.

And it was everything he'd ever wanted.

As soon as they completed the vows, he leaned over and kissed his wife on the lips. "You're mine," he said low enough that only she could hear him.

"I'm yours," she said back to him and he knew she would soon learn the meaning to those words.

The church doors burst open and Mrs. Leake, wearing a dress made of the finest silk, walked in with an army of goons behind her, guns drawn.

"Stop," she said, "that woman belongs to me."

"Slavery went out with the war," Anna said.

"Yes, it did, but you're an indentured servant," the woman replied like she was talking to an imbecile.

"No, I'm not. I didn't sell myself into bondage. My uncle did. Collect from him," she spouted.

The madam approached her, an ugly scowl on her beautiful made-up face. Her hair was an unnatural red, but her figure was the shape every man dreamed of holding. Perfect.

Mack and Jake both drew their guns and stepped in front of Anna.

"I'm her husband and I will protect her with my life, so I suggest you and your guns leave without causing trouble. Or the whole army of Texas Rangers will descend on Blessing and shut you down."

"You married this girl?"

"That's right," Anna said with a grin. "I'm a married woman."

"Anna was being forced into prostitution against her

will, which is against the law. Buying or purchasing or making someone an indentured servant against their will is against the law and we could shut your business down. Do you want to force this issue?" Mack asked. "I can have the sheriff draw up the papers right now to lock your front doors."

The woman growled and stared at Anna with an evil smile and Jake knew that if his wife were to be recaptured, this woman would punish her. The woman had a sick twisted side that Jake didn't like.

"You win for now. But this isn't over, and it would be a shame if she were to become a widow so early in her young life," she said.

Anna laughed out loud. "Or you could find yourself in jail very soon. Now get out of here and stop trying to ruin my wedding."

The woman whirled on her heel and motioned for her guns to follow as she all but stomped up the aisle and out of the church.

When the door slammed, they all stood there for a moment.

"Well, I have never held a wedding quite like this one," the preacher said. "Prayers for your safety and, Mrs. Nash, may your life with your new husband be blessed."

"Thank you, reverend. Now if you'll excuse me, we have a wedding night to get to."

The man's face blushed and Jake did his best not to grin. Anna was going to be a challenge and he couldn't wait to make her theirs.

CHAPTER 7

When they walked into the house, nerves overcame Anna. They were married. Husband and wife and though she had heard and seen things in the brothel, that didn't mean she knew what went on between a man and a woman. Sure she had seen animals copulating, but what happened between a husband and wife, she had no idea.

And she had two husbands. Two men and she had no clue how to handle one.

"Do you still have that dress from the saloon?" Mack asked.

Why did he want to know?

"Yes," she said.

"Go and put it on," Jake said. "We'll be waiting for you."

More nerves awoke within her as she walked into the bedroom, unbuttoned her dress and let the beautiful garment fall to the floor. She hung it up in the wardrobe and then slipped the dress on that would have made her a whore. The outfit was extremely enticing and revealing, men were known to like that sort of thing.

Her body was revealed in a very sensuous way that even had her heart beating a little faster. Her breasts and pussy were covered, but there were slits that revealed her legs when she walked. The bodice was low cut and her breasts almost spilled out, her nipples barely covered.

And you could see the pebbled nubs through the silk.

She walked out of the bedroom into the living room and faced her two men, who stood before her naked. Shock and heat rippled through her and her center ached for something she didn't know.

Their male bodies were strong, their muscles clearly defined, as she gazed at their manhoods hard and rigid. From their kiss, she knew they tasted and smelled different. Jake tasted of the outdoors and Mack like he'd eaten something sweet. Mack smelled of wood smoke while Jake smelled of leather and horses. Both were unique. Both made her heart beat faster.

"Beautiful," Mack said as he stroked his cock.

For a moment, she stared. She'd never seen a man's personal parts and the long member fascinated her. Smooth and rigid and hard and she longed to touch the very end. See how it felt when he slid the skin up and back.

"Now, we're going to rip it off you," Jake said, his eyes darkening with something that reached into her very soul and drew her to him.

Blood heated and pounded as it rushed through her, causing her lungs to squeeze as she gasped for breath at the thought of them stripping her naked.

"We're going to destroy the gown that would have

enslaved you," Mack said, walking close to her, his hand on his cock, stroking it, making it grow longer and harder.

"Then we'll make you ours," Jake said, gazing at her as he stepped close and ripped the white silk and lace down the front exposing her breasts.

Automatically, her hands reached up to cover her flesh from his gaze, a whimper escaped from her throat. He removed her hands and then stepped back to stare at her breasts.

"Anna, they're gorgeous," he said.

Warmth grew in her lower stomach. And yet she felt as nervous as a filly standing there before them.

Anxieties overcame her and she reached up to cover her breasts again.

"No, honey, we're your men and can't wait to see every inch of you," Jake said in a soothing voice. "We're going to taste every inch of you. We're going to love every inch of you tonight."

His words caused her pulse to race, the center of her ached and her breathing to become labored.

"We can't wait to explore your gorgeous body," Mack said as his fingers skimmed over her breasts as he took her nipples between his fingers and twisted them.

A fiery heat spiraled through her and she gasped.

"We want to hear you moan and eventually scream our names," Jake said, moving behind her, whispering in her ear, his breath tickling, causing her to moan.

A rip sounded behind her as the back of the dress came down. Cold air drifted over her skin, but on the inside, she was on fire.

Mack gripped the skirt and ripped it from her body,

exposing her cunny to his gaze. "Oh, Jake, she has a sweet looking pussy."

His hand slid down her chest, past her waist until he reached between her legs, his fingers sliding over her folds.

Pleasure rippled through her and she gasped. "Mack."

"Honey, you're dripping wet," he said. "I think you like your husbands stripping you."

What could she say? The dress was offensive, and yet the way they had rid her of its importance, she enjoyed. It was like they were destroying Mrs. Leake's plans for her.

Another rip sounded behind her and cool air brushed against her backside. The dress was gone and she stood completely nude before them.

For a moment, they stared at her as they walked around her in a circle, gazing at her body. In a way, it made her feel like they cherished her.

Mack stepped in closer to her, his mouth came down on hers as he ravaged her mouth, making her knees grow weak. His tongue pushed its way inside her mouth, and he explored her while his fingers continued to stroke her clit. Never had she felt so many emotions at once.

So much heat.

Fingers trailed down her spine as she felt Jake caressing her backside. "Your ass is beautiful. Nice and firm and I can't wait to fuck you here."

"What?" She broke the kiss, her breathing heavy. Did he just say what she thought he said?

Mack continued to stroke over her pussy lips, slipping a finger inside causing her breathing to almost cease as pleasure filled her. "But my ass?"

"You have two men. We'll prepare you, but eventually,

we'll both take you at the same time," Jake whispered against her ear, his fingers sliding down her crack, touching her in the most private area.

"Oh," she cried as his fingers circled her anus. The shock of feeling pleasure from that area had her standing on her tippy toes trying to escape, yet knowing, she had nowhere to go. And the heat that simple touch created had her gasping.

One man was at her back and the other her front and the friction she felt as their fingers stroked her was almost more than she could bear.

Mack dropped to his knees and she felt his fingers pulling apart her pussy lips and then his mouth was on her, his tongue lapping at her, causing her knees to grow weak as she grabbed his shoulders to keep herself from falling.

"Mack, what are you doing?"

"I'm tasting your cunt and it's sweeter than honey," he said as he began to lick her faster, his tongue pushing up inside her, creating a spasm that had her moaning.

Desire had a strangle hold on her and she could feel the pleasure building inside her, ready to explode and she didn't know how to handle the feeling. Never had she felt such intensity, all centered in her pussy.

Jake eased his finger into her back entrance, insistent and sure. The feel of that finger probing her, swirling and demanding entry, sent her spiraling out of control. She screamed as the world around her shattered. Her men held her as her body tensed and she bucked and felt like she would faint.

Finally, it ended and Jake held her while Mack slowly stood.

"Honey, I think you liked my finger in your ass."

How could he say that, yet it was true. While she felt embarrassed, she'd been unprepared for the feeling of hunger, the insistent need for him to stroke her.

"Did you like it?"

How could she answer him? If she said the truth, he would think she was perverse.

"Always tell us the truth and how you feel."

"Yes," she whispered still not certain what had happened a moment ago.

Mack smiled. "She came all over my face," he said with a grin. "Nothing sweeter."

"What happened," Anna asked as the world began to right, though she felt like she was moving in a fog. While she heard their words, her mind seemed to be moving in slow motion.

"You came," Jake said. "Your first orgasm."

"But not your last of the night," Mack said with a grin as he wiped his face. "We've waited long enough. It's time to make you ours."

Each man took her arm and they led her into the bedroom. They were all naked and she liked the feel of their skin against her own. The warmth, the silk, the hardness of their bodies.

"You get the honors of taking her maidenhead," Jake said as he glanced at Mack who grinned. "Eventually, I get to take her in the ass first."

Jake lay on the bed and had Anna lay on top of him, her back to his chest. His tongue reached out and licked her ear and she moaned. "I'm not going to take your ass tonight, but soon. And, darling, I can't wait for the two of us to take you together. Us filling all your holes."

His words sent a shiver through her. How could they do something so depraved, so dirty, and yet, just the sound of his voice left her heated. Part of her couldn't wait to experience them at the same time and that shocked her.

Mack crawled on the bed over her. She was sandwiched between the two men and she moaned at the feel of their naked flesh against her own. Mack's chest crushed her breasts, his legs long and lean, his mouth inches from her own.

His long, hard dick strutted out in front of him like a sword. Never had she considered two men before and now she couldn't imagine sex any other way. The feel of being sandwiched between them was nothing like she'd ever experienced. It was like they enfolded her into their bodies.

Mack placed his long, rigid penis at the entrance to her pussy and suddenly fear spiraled through her.

"It's all right," Jake said as if sensing her alarm. "It will hurt only for a moment and then Mack and I are going to give you the most intense pleasure you've ever felt. We're going to make you scream with passion, and before the night is over, you'll want us to fuck you every night."

Just the words were enough to cause her breathing to increase and her heart to hammer in her chest.

A whimper escaped her before Mack reached down, parted the folds between her legs, and rubbed the little nub. Pleasure spiked through her and she moaned and lifted her hips as if to urge him to fuck her.

He moved forward and she felt him entering her pussy

while his fingers continued to rub her and she groaned. Then she felt him reach the wall of resistance.

With a quick thrust, he was through. For a moment, he stayed there and didn't move. A sharp pain centered around the stinging area, but then it was over. She groaned as she felt her body accommodate him, stretching to accept his long cock as he filled her.

"Oh my God, you're so big," she whimpered.

"That I am," Mack said. "And now, I'm going to make you scream when you come this time."

With trepidation, she gazed into Mack's eyes and heat exploded inside her when he began to move.

It was the most incredible feeling, and while he went slowly, she suddenly wanted him to hurry.

To move faster.

As soon as he was completely inside her, he pulled out and she raised her hips, needing, wanting more of him inside her. Wanting to scream *put it back*.

Then she felt, Jake's fingers plunging inside her back entrance. With a cry, she rose and met Mack and then dropped down on Jake's fingers. Oh God, she wanted more. Up and down she rode them.

"That's it, sweetheart, open up for me. Take me inside your ass. Let me fill you while Mack fills your pussy. Let us both give you pleasure."

And they were. Never before had she felt such heat and fire building inside her. Jake pushed a second finger inside her rectum and she squealed at the pain-pleasure that exploded inside her. She could feel them going back and forth inside her body, the heat building. The fire raging and then she felt her orgasm like a tsunami roaring toward her.

"Mack," she screamed as she clenched his cock inside her tightly, squeezing it. Waves of pleasure filled her, and for a moment, she felt like she would drown as she gulped for air. He exploded inside her, coating her pussy walls with his seed. Like a butterfly, she drifted back to earth, safe in Jake's arms.

She rolled over to curl up in a ball on the bed and fall asleep, completely relaxed and spent, when she heard a voice. "Anna, we're not finished. You need to take care of Jake."

Oh, she had completely forgotten. And yet, she couldn't wait to experience what his cock would feel like deep inside her.

No, she didn't forget about Jake. In some ways, she couldn't wait to feel Jake. He was the dark one, the mysterious man. The man who when he looked at her, all she wanted to do was remove her clothes.

And he was hers.

She rolled onto her back as Jake stood. "No, I want to take you from behind. I want to see your ass twitch as I shove my cock in your pussy. I want to spank your ass as you come."

The sound of his words left her nervous as she eagerly moved until she was on her hands and knees. She glanced back at Jake and he rubbed his hand over her buttocks. "Sorry, darling, but I want to hear you moan."

He slapped her ass not hard, but with enough force that she felt it jar all the way to her pussy. "Oh, Jake."

"One more time," he said as his hand connected with

her ass. It burned but the heat created a fire inside her. A fire that centered in her middle.

With a sigh, he pushed forward, her head coming to rest on her arms, her ass sticking up in the air.

"Now that's the sight I've been waiting to see. Your cheeks slightly pink from my hand, your pussy dripping with want for me and your ass just begging for my finger."

His words had her moaning.

Mack chuckled. His mouth covered hers as Jake plunged into her waiting cunny. She groaned not from pain, but pleasure as Mack's lips consumed hers while Jake hammered into her, his cock hitting the wall of her womb.

As Mack's kiss commanded her surrender, his lips ravaged hers, his tongue demanding entry, his fingers twisting her nipples. Oh, how she loved the way Mack kissed and the way Jake slammed his cock into her again and again.

She released Mack's lips, needing to draw as much air into her lungs as possible as she felt another orgasm building.

The bed squeaked, the mattress hitting the back wall as Jake pounded into her.

"Don't come," he commanded, and she wondered how he thought she could hold back. The need was building, roaring through her.

She bit her lip, trying to stop the need to explode all over his cock. "I can't…"

Smack! He hit her ass with his palm. He lifted her hips to meet him and she could feel a scream building inside.

"Now. Now, you can come," he cried as his seed exploded inside her, coating her pussy walls.

And she did. A scream tore from her throat as she cried out, "Jake. Oh, Jake."

He held her against him while she writhed and convulsed in his arms. Finally, they collapsed onto the bed. Totally spent, she lay there, knowing she would never be the same. Knowing, she truly belonged to Mack and Jake.

Her men arranged her body until she was between them.

"This is how it will always be. You between the two of us."

"Your needs are what's important to us. We will always take care of you," Jake said.

How much luckier could a woman get than to have two men who looked out for her in her bed every night. Yes, this was her first experience, but she couldn't wait for the next lesson.

CHAPTER 8

*J*ake glanced around the mercantile and wished his wife would finish with her purchases. The last two days had been heaven and he couldn't wait to get her home and strip her naked.

They had not gone anywhere, but stayed in bed, exploring their woman, and listening to her scream with passion. But today, she told them they were running low on food and needed to make a trip to the store.

As she pulled items from the shelves, Mack took them to the counter. Jake refused to leave her side. There were people who would love to hurt her and he wasn't risking her being stolen from them.

His eyes constantly scanned the store and the expression on his face had ladies scurrying away from the two of them.

"Jake, honey, don't frighten the shoppers," Anna said with a laugh. "They don't know that you're easily tamed."

"They also don't know that I would kill to protect you.

Time to finish, Anna. We need to get home before there's trouble."

"I'm married now. No one is going to cause us trouble," she admonished.

"Not even your uncle?"

She sighed. "He could be a problem."

Well, at least the stubborn woman admitted that.

"Exactly. Come on, you're safer at home."

Mack hurried back to them. "Five riders just pulled up to the store. One of whom is Walter Farris."

Shit, the very man they were talking about.

Jake pushed Anna behind him as the men entered the store.

"Good morning, gentlemen," Mr. Bailey, the owner of the mercantile called. "I don't want any trouble in my store."

"Then you shouldn't have let this whore in your establishment," Walter said as he walked over to stand in front of Jake and Mack.

Anger gripped Jake, his fists clenched and the urge to punch the man almost overcame him.

"You just called my wife a whore and those are fighting words," Jake said as he pulled his gun. "Apologize. Besides you're the one who tried to make her into a whore."

The man grinned. "The girl was useless. And why let all this beauty go to waste."

"No, you did it because I learned your secrets," Anna said. "You were trying to keep me quiet."

"Anna, be quiet," Jake said. "Mack and I will handle this."

The uncle frowned. "Time to come home, Anna."

"No, I'm married to a Texas Ranger," she said.

That just earned her a spanking. He had told her to obey him and she would not shut up. He really didn't want the outlaw to know he was a Texas Ranger. They wanted to capture him undercover, but now that would be impossible.

"Anna, shut up," he repeated.

He heard her huff behind him but didn't take his eyes off the man in front of him.

The men in the store begin to circle them and Mack moved to put Anna between them, his back to her back as he pulled his gun out.

"Go get the sheriff," he heard the owner tell his wife.

But one of the men pulled a gun on her halting her footsteps. "Don't move if you want to live."

The woman screamed and ran behind her husband.

"Walter, stop this," the man behind the counter cried. "You will pay if you shoot up my store."

Jake didn't take his eyes off her uncle, ignoring the chaos around him. He wanted the man to know he meant what he said.

"My partner and I are well trained and my first bullet is in your chest. I won't need a second. Is this what you want?"

The man grinned. "Anna owes money to the brothel. You need to return her there, so she can work off her debt."

"That's not true," Anna hollered and Jake knew she didn't understand that when he gave her a command it was to be followed.

"No, you sold her. You pay back the brothel owner. No

wife of mine is ever going to work in a whorehouse. Do you understand me? Anna stays with me."

The men had surrounded them and Mack had both of his guns trained on them.

"What brings two Texas Rangers to town?"

Why was he changing the direction of their conversation? If he cared for his niece, he would be learning more about Jake, but instead, he wanted to know why the rangers were in town. The man didn't love or care for Anna. But she must have something else he wanted.

"What else? The stagecoach robberies. First the masked bandit took the gold, but he made a mistake when he also killed the shotgun rider. He moved from simple robbery to murder," Jake replied.

A woman walked into the store, saw all the guns, screamed and ran back out. That would probably bring the sheriff.

They were in the middle of the store in between the canned goods and Jake knew they were fairly well protected if a gun fight ensued, except for Walter who stood in front of him and one of his hired guns that stood in front of Mack. One bullet would do them in.

If they were going to shoot them, they were running out of time. Somehow he got the feeling that they wanted to intimidate them. See if Walter could convince him to give up Anna. But that wasn't going to happen. Also learn how much they knew about his operation, because Jake was fairly certain that Walter was the masked bandit.

But why would a man who owned a fairly large cattle ranch be robbing stages. That was a question he needed to find the answer to.

"You know if Anna were a widow, she could still go back to work at the whorehouse."

The very thought angered Jake even more. This idiot was severely tempting him to kill him if he didn't shut up.

"My wife is not going to become a widow or a whore anytime soon."

"We'll see about that," the man said with the most evil smile Jake had ever seen. He was cold and ruthless. And then he remembered that Anna suspected him of killing her parents.

Why would he have killed them? He needed to ask her more questions about how they died.

Just then the sheriff walked in the door. The man had blonde curls that hung below his cowboy hat and dark brown eyes that were narrowed. "What's going on here? Some lady ran in and said the mercantile was being robbed."

Walter laughed. "Hardly, sheriff. Just a friendly discussion about my niece."

It was not a friendly discussion and Jake would just as soon kill Walter, but he was a lawman sworn to do what was right.

"The one that's gone missing from the brothel?"

"I did not go there by choice," Anna said.

Would the woman never learn to let him handle the situation?

"My wife will never work in a whorehouse," Jake said.

The sheriff frowned. "Gentleman, I'm sure that Mr. Bailey would like if you didn't frighten his customers. Take it outside. Now, I've got to run."

"Nothing to take outside, sheriff. We're doing some shopping and then we're leaving."

The lawman left the building.

Walter frowned. "This is not over. I will get my niece back one way or the other. If you were smart, you'd get on your horse and ride out of here, but your kind usually aren't too smart."

The words were meant to rile him, but Jake just stared at him, not responding. "No, it's not over. I'm here to find who killed Gerard Jones and is robbing the stages. And you, Mr. Farris, are one of my suspects."

The man laughed. "I don't know what Anna has told you, but you won't find what you're looking for out at the Riverbend Ranch. Just remember that my niece is a little soft in the head and likes to tell lies. That's why I decided she should be a whore."

Jake felt his insides explode with rage. He cocked his gun and the man's eyes widened.

"Careful, that's my wife you're talking about. No one gets away with mistreating her. No one. Do you understand?"

The man's eyes then narrowed. "We'll talk again soon, Ranger." He glanced at Anna. "And you just sealed your husband's fate."

Jake felt Anna move behind him and before he could stop her, she hurled herself at her uncle, her fists doubled. She got one swing in that connected with his nose, causing blood to spurt everywhere, before Jake hauled her back.

"Stop," he hissed in her ear.

"Let me at him," she said kicking and screaming.

"No," Jake said.

Walter grinned an evil twist of his lips as he put a hand-kerchief up to his nose. "Told you, she was crazy."

With a wave of his hand, his guns followed him out the door.

Mack laughed out loud. "Damn, honey, you throw a mean punch. But disobeying just got you in trouble."

CHAPTER 9

Seething with anger, Anna sat between Jake and Mack on the long silent ride home, even though the mercantile was only a few blocks away. She knew they were angry. Furious.

And her hand ached from where she punched her uncle, but the man had it coming.

The back end of the wagon was loaded down with groceries and she couldn't wait to put everything away and cook them a pie or something that would brighten their moods. Right now, she didn't know what they were going to do, but she was fearful.

When they pulled up in the drive, Jake turned to her, his brown eyes dark with anger. "Go in the house, remove your clothes, and wait on the bed for us."

"But I want to put away the supplies."

Mack shook his head. "Woman, unless you want your bottom blistered, I would suggest that you do what he says."

With a sigh, Mack helped Anna alight from the wagon.

"I'll be in the bedroom. Make certain the meat gets stored in the root cellar."

"We've been doing this a lot longer than you think," Jake said.

That probably didn't help her cause as she marched into the house. All she wanted to do was claw her uncle's face. The man had lied about her to her husbands. How could she remain silent when he called her crazy and yet she had acted like a lunatic going for him?

And now her men were angry with her.

Going into the bedroom, slowly she removed her clothes. They refused to let her buy pantaloons today at the mercantile and she didn't understand why. She thought of the nice clothes her uncle had of hers and longed for the things in her bedroom.

He had cost her so much. First her parents, then her normal everyday life and then the trip to the brothel. A shiver went through her. She had a right to want to gouge his eyes out. He'd taken so much from her.

And now she worried about her husbands. Would he make her a widow?

She crawled up on the bed and got on her knees, placing her head on the bed, naked.

The last two days they had been training her to assume the different positions they wanted and this one seemed to be their favorite.

She heard their boots on the stairs and prepared herself for their anger.

They walked into the room and then sank down on the bed. Jake pulled her up to face him. "Did I tell you to be quiet?"

"Yes," she said meekly.

"Did you stop," Jake asked.

"The man has done so much harm to me. I wanted to—"

"Did you tell him we were Texas Rangers?" Mack asked.

Her eyes widened and she realized they may not have wanted him to know they were here in town.

"Yes," she said.

"Now the whole town knows why we're here."

With a sigh, she truly did feel bad about shouting out that they were Texas Rangers, but she was proud of them. Of what they stood for.

"I'm sorry. I wanted him to know I had two strong men protecting me."

"Don't you think he could see that?" Mack replied.

Jake's eyes were still dark with fury. "You disobeyed not once, but twice, and then you sucker punched him."

And it had given her great satisfaction to land that punch. She hoped it broke his nose.

"That part I'm not sorry for," she said. "The rest, you're right. I should have kept my mouth closed. But he called me crazy."

"And then you acted like a crazy woman," Mack said.

It was true, but dang, if it didn't feel good to get at least one punch in before they pulled her off him.

"Didn't we tell you that if you disobeyed us, you would be punished," Jake said.

Her eyes widened as she wondered what they were going to do.

"I'm sorry. I'll do better next time. Being married is new to me."

Jake's brows rose. "It's new for all of us, but you need to

learn the rules now. When either one of us tell you to be quiet, to stop, whatever the command is, you are to obey."

They had warned her that they expected complete obedience and already she'd failed.

"Do you understand," Mack said.

"Yes, but I couldn't today. I just couldn't," she said, knowing that nothing could have stopped her from getting to her uncle. Nothing.

"And so you will be punished," Jake said. "Over my knee."

She bit her lip and tried to look at him in a pleading way. One where maybe he wouldn't punish her, but his jaw was rigid and his gaze was cold. "Now."

Standing, she laid over his lap, her head hanging down, her hair touching the floor. His palm hit her bottom cheeks and not in the playful, sexual way, but in a punishing smack.

"Count your licks," Mack said.

"One," she said with a gasp.

Smack, his palm hit her flesh again, stinging and causing her bottom to burn.

"Two," she said.

Smack, and this time she could feel tears prick her lids.

"Three." She moaned, biting her lip, trying not to cry, but knowing she couldn't take much more.

Smack, the sound reverberated through the room and she cried out.

"Four," she cried.

Smack, tears rolled down her face into her hair and she begin to cry. "You said you would never hurt me."

Jake massaged her cheeks and it was both torturous and

exquisite. "If you don't disobey, then there would be no need to make your punishment hurt. We really only want to give you pleasure, but you have to listen to us."

He pulled her up and took her in his arms. "We only want to protect you. Cherish you."

"Keep you safe, and today, you were not safe," Mack said, wrapping his arms around Anna.

"I hate him," she cried as she clung to Jake. The feel of his chest, his arms wound around her, felt like she was encased in armor. Like nothing could harm her here.

The bed squeaked as Mack got up and began to remove his clothing. Really? He thought she wanted to have sex now? Her bottom was burning, her emotions were all over the place, and she felt humiliated.

She couldn't remember the last time she had ever received a spanking.

When Mack was completely naked, he took her in his arms. "If you obey us, you're safe. We're your men and we're here to take care of you. To fight your battles including the one with your uncle. Depend on us and let us take care of you."

"But I want revenge," she said with a little hiccup.

"No, we're going to take care of your uncle," Mack said.

The bed moved as Jake joined them, nude. He slipped his fingers between her legs and pulled them apart. "You're wet. You didn't like the severity of the punishment, but you did like the spanking. We'll spank you with pleasure and for punishment. Do you understand?"

What could she say? She did like when they had done it while they were having sex, but today Jake had taken it a little further than she cared for.

He reached out and wiped her tears from her face. "Obey us, Anna, and you won't have to experience this kind of punishment again."

"I'm trying," she said.

"You do have one hell of a right hook," Mack said as his hands began to pull at her nipples, sending warmth shooting through her. She gasped as she gazed up at him.

"My father taught me," she said with a smile.

Jake lay on the bed, his cock rigid, a smile on his face. "Suck my cock."

This was something she'd never heard of. "What?"

"Put your lips around my cock and suck on the head," he commanded.

She knew better than to argue with him, so she crawled over the man and then placed her lips around his manhood. Oddly, the skin was smooth as she pulled it into her mouth.

"Now run your tongue around it and suck on the bulb," he said with a moan.

As she sucked on Jake's cock, Mack moved behind her. His fingers teased her clit causing her to tighten around his fingers as they moved over the lips. She moaned and Jake jerked.

"Dear God, do that again," he said.

Mack thrust his fingers up into her pussy and she moaned knowing that soon, they would have her screaming with passion. His hands spread her cheeks and he put his mouth against her pussy and she all but screamed.

"Oh, that feels good," Jake said.

Mack's hands gripped her hips as he let his tongue

work magic on her clit, her pussy lips and even swirling that sweet instrument up inside her. She groaned as heat spread through her like a volcano building to explosion.

Jake grabbed her head and pushed his cock farther in her mouth, and for a moment, she feared she was going to choke, but instead he moved her head up and down.

"I'm going to come in your mouth, Anna. Swallow it all," he said as he groaned, his body going rigid as he shoved his cock deep in her throat. She felt his seed filling her mouth.

It didn't taste bad, but all she could think about was the way that Mack's mouth was doing to her what she had done to Jake. Then he pulled his mouth away and he moved behind her. She leaned back, eager to feel his cock in her pussy.

He met her and slammed into her pussy and she groaned at the feel of him stretching her, filling her as she moved her hips to accommodate him. For a moment, they moved in unison as he held her hips, rocking her exactly like he wanted.

Then she felt his finger twirling around her back passage. Rubbing the heat of their passion over the tiny hole, then plunging his finger inside. She gasped at the heat that consumed her.

Why did this feel so good? Why did it seem so depraved and yet she wanted more? She pushed back eager to feel his fingers plummet into her again, but instead it was a second finger.

"Oh," she cried as he began to stretch her even farther.

"Relax, Anna, let me in. Let me fuck you with my fingers," Mack said.

She tried, but when he added a third finger, she moaned. "Mack, I don't think I can do it."

Jake reached for her nipples and twisted them. "You're going to take more than his fingers eventually. Soon you're going to take our cocks."

His mouth covered hers as Mack, plunged three fingers in her and she moaned in Jake's mouth and yet the feeling was more and intense fullness. Heat shot through her as Jake all but chewed her lip off.

Between the two of them, they were sending her spiraling toward the edge.

She released Jake's mouth. "I'm going to come."

"Not yet, you're not," Mack said, and he slapped her ass, but this time between the two of them, it was more pleasure than pain.

"Mack," she cried as she bit her lip to keep from coming.

Pulling his fingers out of her ass, he inserted them in and twisted one more time.

"Now, you can come," he said as he slammed his cock against her womb, his seed spilling against the walls.

She screamed with pleasure, her body shaking and undulating as the orgasm rocked her over and over, plunging her headfirst over a cliff only to land safely in her husband's arms.

Mack and Anna collapsed onto the bed. The two men moved her until she was between them.

"This is where you belong," Jake said as she slowly recovered. "This is how we will always protect you."

"If you disobey us, you will be punished," Mack said, gasping for breath.

They lay in silence as they all three seemed to catch their breath.

Finally, Jake stood and walked to a dresser nearby. He opened the drawer and pulled something out and brought it back to her.

"It's time we shaved you," he said. "And then we're going to introduce you to butt plugs."

"What is a butt plug?"

"It will prepare you to take both of us at the same time. It's something you wear in your ass to spread your muscles to accept us."

Rising, she gazed at the two men. "Do all married couples have this kind of sex life? Because I never would have imagined my parents doing this."

Mack laughed. "Probably not, honey. We like to live for pleasure. Yours and ours."

With a sigh, she lay down while Jake prepared a cup full of shaving cream and a razor.

"Spread your legs, darling," Jake said.

At least she was back to *darling*. He didn't seem angry like before.

She spread her legs and he rubbed the brush between her legs, stroking her lips.

"Oh," she cried as new tremors filled her body.

"What are you doing with the razor?"

"I'm going to make that pussy shine," he said. "No more hairs."

"Jake," she said.

"Relax," he told her. "I'll make it good for you. Each time the brush touches you, you'll feel pleasure."

And oh, she did. Every time the bristles brushed against

her little nub, she groaned. She wasn't afraid of the razor, just the feel of the brush held her in its grip.

In a matter of strokes, she was shocked at the outcome. Her pussy glistened with Mack's seed and she could see the lips peeking out.

"Now for the butt plug," Mack said, rising from the bed. She watched him go to the same chest and open a drawer.

"Up on your knees," Jake demanded.

Slowly, she turned over and crawled onto her knees. He pushed her head down until her ass was in the air. Then she felt his fingers stroking her clit, pushing into her pussy.

"Jake," she moaned, "make me come."

"Not yet. The best is yet to come," he said and slapped her pussy.

A scream tore from her throat. Not one in pain, but pure pleasure. "Oh, do it again."

And he did.

A finger pushed something cold and gooey into her ass and then spread her hips, exposing her back passage for her men's gaze.

"Relax, Anna," Mack said. "This is the first one. The smallest one, but soon, you won't need them."

"Hurry, I want to fuck her," Jake said.

First, Mack pushed his fingers into her and when he removed them, he pushed the wooden dowel inside.

"Mack," she cried. "It won't fit."

"Yes, it will. Deep breaths. We're almost there."

She felt her body stretching to accommodate the wooden plug.

Pressure filled her back passage and she took deep

breaths, trying to relax, but it felt like someone was pushing a log into her backside.

"All in," Mack said and gave her a smack on the ass, causing the plug to vibrate.

"On your back and spread your legs," Jake commanded.

He pushed into her and she welcomed his cock, but now there was an extra fullness. She was filled in front and the back and she moaned at the exquisite feeling of being consumed.

"Jake," she groaned as Mack twisted her nipples and then leaned in to kiss her, his mouth ravaging hers. His lips taking possession of her. She was helpless. They were her masters and she was all theirs to do with as they wished.

Once again, she was swept up in a firestorm of feelings as desire overwhelmed her. Once again, her men were taking her to the cliff and hanging her over the edge, dangling her there.

"Oh," she cried into Mack's mouth as his tongue ravished her. He broke the kiss and she screamed, "Please, Jake, let me come."

He raised her legs and over her shoulder as he pounded into her pussy and then he smacked the butt plug.

"Now you can come," he said as he hit it sending vibrations through her again and this time it sent her over the edge of the cliff.

"Jake," she screamed as Mack gathered her in his arms and she disintegrated.

$\mathcal{M}$ack lay next to Anna, her naked flesh against his and he couldn't remember the last time he felt this good. He missed his family, his brothers and sisters, and for the first time, he felt like he'd found a place he could call home.

A place where he could settle down and raise a family of his own that he would share with Jake and Anna. A place filled love and laughter and happiness. Maybe he was crazy for wanting such a home, but he needed that sanctuary in his life once again.

But he also knew that right now this situation with Anna was tenuous. He couldn't keep his hands off of her or his cock from swelling every time he thought about her, but there were demons lurking between all of them.

Demons that needed to be removed. His homesickness and Jake's grief and even Anna's loss. They all three needed to heal before they brought a child into their home.

Maybe it was time to ask questions that would hopefully bring them the happiness they all seemed to want. The happiness they'd been waiting for, for so long.

"Tell me why you think your uncle killed your parents."

"They were murdered and the only person who would benefit from their deaths was my uncle. My grandfather passed several months earlier, and Papa inherited the ranch. But the will stated if my father died before I married and had children, then the ranch went to me. My uncle had custody of me."

"So Walter is your mother's brother?" Mack asked, trying to clarify everything in his mind.

"Yes," she said, snuggling in a little deeper.

Jake rolled over and wrapped his arms around her, pulling her in close. For a moment, Mack was jealous. Why hadn't he thought to do that? Instead, he moved in closer and kissed her on the forehead.

"How did they die?" Jake asked.

She pressed her lips together and sighed. "A single gunshot to the head. They were found on the road leading into town. My mother's wedding ring was taken, but nothing else."

A tear trickled down her cheek. "He had to kill them both or my mother would have inherited the ranch."

Anger rose inside of Mack at her loss. "What did the sheriff say?"

She laughed. "It was the old sheriff, not Mr. Ingram. He said they had no way of knowing who killed them. He refused to listen to my suspicions and blew them off as the disturbed grief of a young woman. And then they gave custody of me to my uncle."

"You didn't have any brothers or sisters?" Mack asked.

"No, I'm an only child," she said. "Not even any cousins."

Mack couldn't imagine a life without a house full of kids. He had ten brothers and sisters and he missed each one of them. But for a trusted family member to kill your parents and the law to place you in their custody, that had to be a tough situation.

"Did you ever tell your uncle you thought he killed your parents?" Jake asked.

"Not until he took me to the brothel. Then in a fit of rage, I said everything and that's when he started calling me crazy. Loco. That grief had warped me after the death of my parents. One night not long before Papa and Mama were killed, I heard him and Papa arguing one night. Uncle Walter wanted Papa to give him money to go looking for gold. Papa said no."

They were silent as they lay there in bed, Mack letting her words settle inside him, letting his anger build, but also trying to look at what she'd told them from every angle as a Texas Ranger.

The cause was obvious and yet he needed proof before he could arrest the man. Proof that showed he was the killer. Proof that tied him to the gold robberies.

"If the man, as your guardian, had control of the family ranch, why would he be stealing the gold shipments from the stage," Jake asked. "Was the ranch in trouble?"

"Not that I know of," she said curling into Jake.

"We need to talk to the banker," Mack said, spooning around her back, pressing his cock between her legs.

She flipped around and gazed at Mack. "Uncle Walter

67

and he are friends. But I never thought anything about it. Mr. Elam was friends with my father as well."

"Mr. Elam is the banker?"

"Yes," she said as she wound her body around his, pressing her pussy into his cock.

"Do you never get enough," Jake said grinning.

"You're the ones who taught me," she said with a sigh. "Oh, how I wanted brothers and sisters. Did you have brothers and sisters?"

An ache built in Mack's chest at the thought of his own family. Oh, how he missed them.

"Ten. A houseful of laughter and love until I told my father I was leaving to become a Texas Ranger. Then he got mad."

"Why?"

"Fear. My mother said he was terrified I was going to get myself killed. I really miss all the love and laughter that was in that house. That's why I'm hoping soon that this house, or wherever we live, we'll soon have the sound of a baby crying and the pitter patter of little feet."

Anna's face softened as she stared at him. "You want children?"

"Of course, I do," he said grinning. "The sooner the better."

She whirled around and cuddled up around Jake. "What about your family? I know so little about either one of you besides the fact that you're lawmen."

"I used to have a sister, but she's dead," he said, his tone flat as he gazed away.

"I'm sorry," she said. "Do you want children?"

He turned and faced her. "Yes, with you. But first we have a job to do."

"Right now?"

"Yes, right now," he said rising. He reached over and lifted her onto her hands and knees, his cock plunging into her pussy. His lips moved over her back and Mack watched as her blue eyes darkened.

"Oh, Jake," she groaned.

"Hey, don't leave me out," Mack hollered as he rose and moved to where his cock was in front of her lips.

She grinned at him. "I could never forget you."

A smack to her ass had her turning to look at Jake. "Squeeze my cock."

"After I suck on Mack," she said her eyes dark as she put her mouth over his cock.

The feel of her lips wrapped around him had him laying his head back against the headboard. Jake smacked her on the ass again, but this time, she didn't move. This time she groaned around Mack's cock.

"Do that again, Jake. I think she likes it," he said with a moan.

Jake plunged his cock into her wet dripping pussy and when he pulled back, he slapped her on the ass again.

She groaned around his cock as she licked the head. The vibration from her moans and the swirling feel of her tongue around the head had him gripping her head, pulling her down farther onto his hard cock.

"I'm going to come, darling. Be sure you swallow every drop," he said with a groan.

A moan escaped from her and he glanced up to see Jake

pulling the butt plug from her ass, twisting it and then pushing it back in.

The woman moaned, her ass wiggling back toward Jake.

Unable to hold off any longer, Mack shoved his cock deeper, his seed coating her throat.

Just as he finished, she pulled her lips from his cock, licking it as she gasped. "Jake, please."

"What is it you want?"

"Please, let me come," she cried.

He pulled the butt plug almost free and then he shoved it back in again. Anna cried out not in pain, but in pleasure as she clenched the sheets on the bed.

Mack slid down and took her in his arms, knowing she would soon shatter in a million pieces and he wanted to hold her, watch her.

"You may come," Jake said as his cock plunged into her pussy and his fingers squeezed her clit. The woman screamed her orgasm, gasping for air as she clung to Mack.

Jake gripped her hips, bringing her pussy up to his cock as he held her there. With a grunt, his seed exploded out into her womb as he released her and then fell on top of her on the bed.

"Damn, woman," he gasped. "You're going to be the death of me."

She rolled over and gazed up at him. "Does that mean you like it?"

"Hell, yes," he said as his mouth covered hers.

ake hated going off and leaving Anna alone, but knew they needed to finish the investigation. Plus Christmas was less than a week away and he'd really like this to be finished before the holidays.

This year he wanted their first Christmas to be special.

This morning, she insisted on them going out to the woods and cutting down a small cedar tree for her to decorate. Every home needed a tree and when she smiled at him, he would give her the moon and the stars to see her happy.

Already she had been planning their Christmas dinner and what she would fix, and the holiday was days away.

But Jake feared that if they didn't catch her uncle, something would happen to her and after the last few days, he couldn't live without her.

She stood in the doorway, that sassy smile on her face that he knew was nothing but pure trouble. "Be careful and hurry home. I'm fixing an apple pie this afternoon."

Mack groaned. "Woman don't tempt me, or I will smear that pie all over you and lick it off."

Tilting her head, she grinned. "Maybe I should make two."

Jake shook his head, worry filling him. How could they keep her safe? "Lock the doors and stay inside. Do not open the door to anyone."

"We should get you a pistol," Mack said with a frown.

"I'm quite adept with a frying pan," she said. "Now go, so you can come back to me. Maybe I'll be wearing only my apron."

"That just earned you a swat on the ass," Mack said. "Now I have to think about you all day wearing just an apron."

She grinned. "Bye, my husbands."

Mack watched her shut the door. "She is a tempting morsel."

"That she is," Jake said as he turned his horse, unable to listen to her tease them any longer. They had a job to do. Catch the masked bandit, and hopefully, he was connected to her uncle.

"Let's go by the bank before we wait on the stage," Jake said. "I want to talk to this Mr. Elam."

"Let's go," Mack said, still glancing back at the house. "Maybe one of us should stay."

"We have a job. Let's do it. Her pussy will still be there when we get home."

Mack grinned at him. "Damn, I'm glad we married her."

"Me too," Jake said as he rode his horse down the residential street, looking around to make certain they weren't being watched. "Do you see anyone on the street?"

"No," Mack said. "Damn, I hope the stage comes in on time today."

In fewer than ten minutes, they pulled their horses up in front of the bank. An old brick building, it wasn't very large with steps leading to the wooden doors. They tied their horses to the railing and then hurried up the steps.

When they walked in, two tellers sat in cages while a man sat outside an office with a brass plaque over the door. Mr. Elam, Bank President.

"There's his office," Mack said.

They walked up to the man sitting outside the office. "We'd like to speak to Mr. Elam," Jake said.

The man frowned. "What do you need to speak to him about?"

"We're Texas Rangers," Mack said, frowning at the young man whose eyes had grown large.

They had a job to do and Mack wasn't about to take any sass from a young up-and-coming banker.

"Let me see if he's available," he said, rising from his chair.

He knocked and then opened the door and shut it behind him. In a matter of moments, he came back. "Mr. Elam will see you."

"Thank you," Mack said in a sarcastic tone that made Jake smile. His partner was often the more gracious of the two, but there was a side of him that refused to put up with bullshit.

Their boots clomped on the wooden floor as they entered the bank president's office.

"George Elam," he said, standing and holding out his hand. The rounded man looked like a typical banker wearing a suit with a string tie, his fat jowls making his face look long. His hair was receding, but he wasn't bald yet. Give him a few more years and he'd be there.

"Jake Nash and Mack Savage, Texas Rangers."

"Have a seat. How can I help you gentleman?" he said, sitting and giving them the *I've done nothing wrong* smile. Anyone who worked in law enforcement long enough came to recognize the grin.

The office was richly furnished with burnished oak. A large desk had a few scattered papers on it, and a painting of Texas bluebonnets hung on the wall.

"We're here in town investigating the stagecoach robberies. Can you tell me if the gold was meant for your bank?"

"Yes, we receive a shipment about once a month."

"So you've had six shipments stolen from you in the last year?"

"Actually, it's been eight. I've barely been able to keep the bank going. I'm so glad to hear that you men are on the case. Especially, after that shotgun rider was killed."

The man seemed sincere. Jake was a pretty good judge of character and this man seemed honest. Or he was very good at lying.

"Do you know anyone who would be stealing from the bank? Who would go after the gold?" Mack asked.

The man frowned and steepled his hands together. "No, I've thought about it and pondered who I might have made angry, but the only person who comes to mind is the sheriff."

Jake frowned. "Why him?"

It seemed odd that he would pick out law enforcement.

Unless he wanted to cast aspersions on him in order to keep the sheriff from investigating the banker.

"Oh, he's new in town. Used to be a Texas Ranger until the last sheriff resigned. He keeps us all honest, that's for certain."

Wasn't that a sheriff's job?

"But why is he angry at you?"

"Don't rightly know. I helped him solve the case he was working on. You'd think he would owe me, but he let me know right away that he isn't beholding to anyone."

This was all news to Jake. He didn't know that another ranger lived here in town. They would need to speak to him and see what he could tell them. They had briefly met the sheriff at the mercantile the day after their marriage but knew nothing about him. Maybe it was time to pay him a little visit.

They stood to leave and suddenly Jake remembered. "Oh, did you know Thomas and Ida Best?"

"Lovely couple. What a tragedy and it seems like their daughter Anna is now out of her mind with grief. She's throwing around all kinds of accusations about her uncle Walter. Really nice family. What a shame."

Mack tilted his head. "In town, it's rumored that the uncle sold her to the brothel. Is that true?"

The man made a face that appeared aghast at the news.

"Never. She ran off to the brothel and now she's telling all these lies," the banker said shaking his head. "Who would have known that she would turn out to be such a tramp."

Anger sizzled along Jake's spine like a snake curling and

ready to strike. His fists clenched and he had to remind himself not to react.

"Watch what you say," Jake said, his voice low and dangerous. "She's my wife."

The man's jaw dropped, and he stared at them with shock. And Jake knew he was a liar.

"Good day, gentleman," he said as he recovered.

They walked out the door. Neither of them said a word until they were on their horses and riding. "Let's speak to the sheriff."

Mack shook his head. "Until he started talking about Anna, I believed him. Now, I'm questioning everything he said."

"That's why I want to speak to the sheriff," Jake said.

They tied their horse to the hitching post in front of the sheriff's office. As they walked up the steps, they noticed the wanted posters hanging out in front. When they were in Waco, they received briefings on the latest criminals, but it had been over two months since they had visited the home office. The life of a ranger was always being on the road to catch the next criminal.

When they opened the door, a tall dark haired man stood from behind a desk. "Good morning. Seth Ingram, sheriff. What can I do for you?"

Jake liked the man immediately. He seemed like an honest man. "Jake Nash and Mack Savage, Texas Rangers."

The man smiled. "I was a Texas Ranger until my son was born and then I decided to stay closer to home. The town needed a sheriff and here I am."

The thought of going off and leaving Anna alone with a baby on the way or even their children running around gave Jake a moment of angst. He didn't want to leave her. He understood exactly why this man had chosen his family over his profession. But what would he do?

"Once a ranger, always a ranger," Mack said, grinning at the man.

"Have a seat gentleman and tell me what brings you to town."

Jake needed to feel the man out before he confessed what he knew.

"Tell me about your relationship with Mr. Elam, the banker. We were just over there talking about the stagecoach robberies," Jake said.

The man leaned back. "Those stagecoach robberies are being done by someone here in town. Wait a minute. You're the man that married Anna Best."

"Yes, I married her."

"Congratulations."

"Thank you," Jake said, and he wondered how Mack felt not being able to say he was her husband too.

Seth frowned and shook his head. "You saved her life. Mrs. Leake is not a good woman. And I have suspicions that someone else is the owner of the brothel and she just runs it, but I haven't been able to find out who just yet."

Mack sat forward. "Anna says that her uncle sold her to that brothel."

The sheriff nodded. "I'm not surprised. Let me tell you everything I know about what's going on in this town. My partner, Will Parker, and I cleaned up a cattle rustling operation, but I think maybe there are other things afoot here in town that aren't right."

Jake felt better that he was telling them everything he knew.

"The stagecoach robberies started nine months ago. Not too long after we broke up the cattle rusting operation and ran the old sheriff out of town. The law here was as crooked as they come. It's odd that no one in town has shown to be any richer. It's like they're sitting on that gold. But why? Then last week, Anna Best was abducted from the brothel. Do you know anything about that?"

"She did not go into that brothel on her own," Mack said.

"Someone dropped her on our doorstep in a potato sack with a note that said Merry Christmas," Jake said. "She was dressed for the auction they were going to hold that night."

The sheriff frowned. "Who could have done that? I really thought it was you boys."

"No, not us," Mack said.

"All right, since we're coming clean, let me tell you what we know. Anna told us that the reason her uncle sold her to the brothel was to keep her quiet. She went snooping and found boxes of gold in his safe. He caught her in the act and instead of killing her, he sold her to the brothel."

The sheriff frowned. "Sounds like Walter Farris is our masked bandit. But why?"

"That's what we're wondering," Mack said.

"They said she ran off and joined the brothel. Said she was crazy with grief over her parents. But they've been dead for two years," the sheriff said with a sigh.

It didn't make sense. Jake shook his head. "Exactly and

she also suspects her uncle of killing them to gain full control of the ranch."

"Then why does he need the gold?" the sheriff asked.

"And is he truly the masked bandit?" Mack said.

Jake pulled out his pocket watch. "We better go if we're going to try to catch him robbing the stage that's due today."

The sheriff grinned at them. "Want some help?"

"Sure, we could always use an extra gun," Mack said.

The sheriff grabbed his hat and coat off the rack and followed them out the door.

CHAPTER 12

*a*nna had just taken the pies out of the oven when she thought she heard a horse. Maybe her men were returning early. She truly hoped so, because she wanted them to see how she had decorated their little home.

The Christmas tree had bows with strings of popcorn. She'd also found some red yarn and cut out pinecones on paper and hung them from the tree.

No, it wasn't the grand decorations her mother always used, but she truly hoped that someday she would get to use those again. Someday she hoped she had her home back.

A knock on the door startled her. Her men wouldn't knock, and they told her not to open the door. Who knew she was here, besides her uncle's guns. And it would be a cold day in hell before she opened the door to them.

She walked into the front area of the house and peeked out the window. It was the banker. What in the world was the banker doing here?

"Anna, open up, it's George Elam. I need to tell you something about your grandfather's will. It's the reason your parents were killed."

How in the world would he know about her grandfather's will? Her heart pounded in her chest and she was tempted to let him in, just to hear what he had to say.

"Open up, Anna. I'm not going to hurt you."

She looked up and down the street to see if she could see any other men, her uncle or any of his hired guns. Yes, she was curious, but she didn't want to disobey Jake and Mack. They would be so angry with her if she disobeyed them again.

And she liked when they were happy with her.

"I'm sorry, but my husband told me not to open the door," she called through the doorway.

"Look, I need to tell you something you don't know. The reason why you were sold to the brothel. The reason your parents are dead. The reason your uncle is doing what he's doing."

Oh, yes, she wanted the answers to all those questions and more, but if she opened the door, then she would be disobeying her men.

"Come back when my husband is here," she said.

The sound of a gun hammer being cocked could be heard from where she was standing. Fear gripped her chest and her heart hammered. A gun fired and she heard the lock break.

The man was crazy. He refused to take no for an answer.

Running into the kitchen, she grabbed a frying pan, her only weapon.

"Where are you?" he called. "Come out here, you little bitch. I don't give a shit that you're married."

It was all she could do not to scream at him. Why was he calling her a bitch if he wanted to be her friend?

She heard him walking through the house, kicking the doors open and knew it was only a matter of time before he found her in the kitchen.

Quietly she moved across the floor and shut the kitchen door, slamming a chair up under the doorknob. She knew it wouldn't hold. It wouldn't last long and she needed to somehow leave a message for her men in case she was taken.

She grabbed the flour and spilled it out on the counter. Hopefully, the banker would never see her scribblings as she drew the letters in the white powder.

Banker. Help.

Suddenly the wooden door splintered, and he reached through the hole to move the chair away. She brought the skillet down on his hand.

The man screamed, curse words flowing from his mouth.

"I told your uncle to kill you, but he refused to listen to me. You're a dead woman now," he cried as his body slammed into the door and it shattered into a million pieces. Like a monster, he stood there with a gun in his hand. "Put the pan down and come out of there."

"No," she said, knowing that if she did, she was a dead woman.

"If I have to come in there, your death will be even more painful and slow. Now get out here," he screamed.

She glanced around the kitchen looking for anything

besides the skillet she could use on this man. But found nothing, but her gorgeous apple pie still warm from the oven.

Without thinking, she grabbed the pie plate and threw it at him. The apple pie hit him in the face, the steaming hot liquid scalding his cheeks.

A scream tore from his throat and his hands flew to remove the hot sugary syrup from the pie. While he couldn't see, she tried to slip past him to run out the door, but at the last second, he grabbed her arm.

"Not so fast, you little she devil. We've got business," he said as he grappled with her.

She swung a punch at him, but he grabbed her wrists.

"You're done. You're coming with me, now," he said, "before your husband comes back."

Her husbands. Her men. They would see the destruction and know she didn't go willingly. That she fought hard not to be taken.

"Now are you going to tell me about my grandfather's will?"

"I'm telling you nothing, you little whore. This time, I'm going to kill you myself," he said. He took her yarn she was using to make Christmas ornaments and wrapped it tightly around her wrists.

Once they were outside, he shoved her toward the wagon.

"Crawl up in the back like a good little whore, so I don't shoot you right here in town," he commanded.

Once again, she found herself in the back of a wagon, being covered. Knowing this was her last chance, she started to scream as loud as her lungs would allow, hoping her men were nearby.

"You bitch," he said and hit her in the head, her last thoughts of Jake and Mack.

Darkness overcame her.

CHAPTER 13

*M*ack couldn't wait to get home to their wife. It had been a frustrating day ending with them waiting for the stage that never materialized. No stage, no masked bandit, and no answers from either the banker or the sheriff.

But at home, Anna would be waiting and she promised to cook them an apple pie. What could be better than a beautiful woman, a great meal, and an evening spent fucking their wife?

As they rode up, Mack froze.

"Damn, the front door's open," Mack said, jumping off his horse and pulling out his gun at the same time.

"We told her to stay inside," Jake said, his voice angry.

"Look at the lock," Mack said as he noticed the way the doorknob hung from the door. A sick feeling flooded his stomach as he entered. Inside, the house was decorated for Christmas and the memory of his mother and the kids all together putting up the tree for the holiday overcame him.

A wave of homesickness washed over him. Not now. Not when he had to look for clues.

He tried to push it aside as they spread out through the house, their guns at the ready. But Mack knew the house was empty. Someone had taken Anna.

When he reached the kitchen, he stared at the destruction. This is where the final battle took place. The floor was covered with apple pie and he knew she'd thrown it at whomever attacked. Glancing at the broken chair, he realized she'd tried to barricade herself in the small room. The door was splintered into a thousand pieces.

Flour was strewn on the counter and then he noticed the words scratched in the white powder. "Jake, look at this."

Jake came running into the kitchen, his face grew red as he gazed at the destruction. "She put up quite a fight."

"That she did, but look in the flour," Mack said, pointing to the counter.

"Banker," Jake read. "Son of a bitch."

"She was trying to let us know who took her," Mack said.

"Could the banker and her uncle be working together?"

"That could be why the gold hasn't been spent in town," Mack said.

"Now that he knows she's married to Texas Rangers, if the banker is involved, he'll be terrified of her telling us about the gold shipments. If he kills her, we have no proof," Jake said. "We've got to find her."

"Not to mention the son of bitch has our wife. Fuck that," Mack said as terror gripped his insides. Nothing could happen to Anna. They had just found her, and he was not about to let anyone harm her.

"Let's go."

A sense of urgency and pure fear had Mack all but running for the door. If they were going to save their bride's life, they needed to find her and quick.

"Where do you think the banker would take her?"

"Probably back to her uncle's if they are working together," Jake said. "That's where we'll start."

"No, he'll expect us there," Mack said.

Jake stopped. "The brothel. He'd take her back to the brothel."

Running out the door, they jumped on their horses. They had a brothel to visit.

CHAPTER 14

*a*nna could not believe the banker returned her to the brothel, though she was hidden in one of the upstairs rooms. Tied to a chair, her feet and wrists were bound. The banker had tied her up and left her upstairs.

It was the fancy suite where married men copulated with their mistresses for an hourly fee. At least they wouldn't kill her here. It would leave a mess in the highest priced room.

The door opened and her nemesis walked in.

"And you're back," Mrs. Leake said with an evil grin. "Being married didn't protect you from me."

Oh, it really did, but what the woman didn't realize was that her husbands would hunt her down.

"My husband will be here soon," Anna said, hoping they would see her message. They were smart men. They would understand and hopefully realize where he took her.

The woman laughed. "It won't matter, because by the time he finds you, you'll be dead."

"George has already sent for your uncle. And this time,

he told him to finish you off. Once you're dead, there will not be a witness to the gold shipments."

The madam knew about the gold? That must mean she was in on the stealing. Time to spread some doubt and fear in her, but also to glean as much information from the whore as she could.

Anna jerked. "Do you really believe that the banker and my uncle are going to share that gold with you?"

The woman walked across the room and slapped her in the face. "Of course, they will. George and I are planning on living on the beaches of Mexico."

Well, that just confirmed they were all three sharing the gold. The stupid woman didn't realize she had just confessed. Now Anna just had to live long enough to tell Jake and Mack.

A chuckle escaped from Anna as she stared in disbelief at the woman. "You really think he's going to leave his wife and kids for you."

Doubt flickered in the woman's eyes. "Yes, he promised me we would walk the sandy shores of the gulf together."

"My uncle promised me a stallion stud horse, too, when my parents were killed. I've yet to see it."

It was true. She wanted to start breeding their mares with a stronger bloodline and her uncle agreed, but never found her a good stallion or gave her the money to find one on her own. After her parents died, he was very tight with the money. And she never understood why.

"Men only listen with regards to one thing. What's between your legs."

An idea began to form in Anna's head. Though she didn't know if the aging madam would agree to it.

"You know, you're going to get caught," Anna said. "My husband is a Texas Ranger and his partner is as well. They are here to catch the criminals robbing the stage."

"I'm not robbing the stage," she said as she walked the floor, the wooden slates creaking.

The gold wallpaper in the room with red velvet finishes reflected the light from the lantern. Though it was still the middle of the day, the curtains were tightly closed.

"No, but you're an accomplice. You knew enough about the plot that they are giving you a third."

The woman was silent.

"If you hand me over to my husband when he comes, I'll put in a good word for you. Tell him you actually stopped them from killing me."

"Why would I do that? I'm about to go to Mexico with my lover and we're going to take with us over a million dollars in gold. I'll never have to lay on my back again."

The thought of sleeping with the banker was enough to almost make Anna gag. Short and round with beady eyes and little hands that made her shudder with disgust at the thought of him touching her. And this woman was stealing to spend her life with him.

She shuddered.

"It's just an offer to see if you were interested in being saved from having to spend time behind bars. Where there are no fancy bedrooms and instead of laying on your back for the banker, it will be the prison guards."

The madam's face flushed and she charged Anna. "You little bitch. I'm not going to prison. I'll die before anyone takes me."

With a shrug of her shoulders, Anna gazed up into the

woman's enraged face. "My husband will find me. He will go after everyone who harmed me, including you. Your business will be closed after he learns that I was brought and held here against my will."

"It won't matter, you'll be dead by then," she said.

And that was a huge fear. That last little exchange didn't get her anywhere except to learn that she was going to die. And soon.

"Your uncle should be arriving and then just like your parents, you will be found tragically murdered. Too late to be saved."

The woman knew about her parents being killed. Did she have a part in their deaths as well? Anna couldn't stop herself from asking.

"Why were my parents killed?"

"Your father overheard your uncle and the banker making plans."

"And that was reason to kill them?"

The woman crossed the room and glanced out the window. "Here comes your uncle now. Ask him. Learn from him why they were killed."

Mrs. Leake walked over and gazed down at her. "Shame you were wasted. What a fine whore you would have made."

Another shudder went through Anna.

"Not what I wanted to do with my life," Anna said as she glared up at the woman. "And the offer to help you is withdrawn. As far as I'm concerned, you can rot in hell with your disgusting lover."

The woman's eyes darkened, and for a moment, Anna feared she would hit her again. But instead she gave her a wicked smile. "Enjoy hell, Anna."

"Fuck you," she responded.

The woman walked out the door, and a few moments later, her uncle walked in.

In so many ways, he looked like her mother, but their personalities were completely different.

"Damn it, Anna, why can't you behave?"

"What fun would that be? I like screwing up your plans. What's the gold for, Uncle?"

She wanted to remind him that they were family. He may be going to kill her, but she would dog him until the very end that they were blood relatives.

"Mind your own business."

"The madam was telling me about her and the banker's plans to run off to Mexico with the gold. Are you sure they're going to let you keep your share?"

"Shut up, Anna," he growled. "You don't know what you're talking about."

"Why? Aren't you going to kill me just like you killed my parents Your own sister and brother-in-law?"

His eyes narrowed and his fists seem to clench. "Your father would not keep his mouth shut. Kind of like you. And now I'm going to be forced to get rid of you as well. And I know the perfect way."

From behind his back, he pulled a rag out and covered her face and nose. Anna tried not to breathe, but eventually her lungs were gasping for air.

And she took one deep breath as darkness ascended.

CHAPTER 15

*J*ake stormed into the bordello, his eyes taking in the scantily clad women, the men at the bar and the missing Mrs. Leake.

Music played from a tinny piano as the whores either lounged on couches or they danced with one another or a man. Most of them were showing off their wares.

A whore came up and draped her arms around him. "Looking for some company, cowboy."

If only she knew that he was about to shut this place down for good.

He removed her arms and glared at her. "Where is Mrs. Leake?"

The woman shrugged and moved away. Jake was tempted to pull out his gun and start firing shots but knew that could be dangerous to innocents. But damn, he wanted his wife back, now.

"Mrs. Leake, get your ass out here now, or I will shut you down," he yelled.

Anger rode him hard and right now all it would take

was one small transgression and he would lose control. His heart was aching and fear drove him. They would kill his Anna, so he had to find her.

The music that had been playing suddenly stopped. The whores all ran to the back and only the men at the bar remained. Many of them, suddenly paid for their drinks and quietly slunk out the door.

The woman appeared at the top of the stairs. "What the hell do you think you're doing?"

"I'm here for my wife," he told her.

"She's not here," she said with a grin. "I haven't seen her since that day at the chapel."

Jake knew she was lying. From the grin on her face, he could tell she thought she had bested him, but he wasn't done.

"Ladies," he said, gazing around at the women who had gathered in a corner. He pulled out his wallet and yanked out money. "I'll pay you one hundred dollars if you'll tell me the truth. Have you seen Anna here today?"

Mack stood beside him watching everything, his hand on his gun, ready to fight.

The girls whispered and while they were trying to decide how to answer, a young girl of about sixteen stepped out. "Put me on the next stage out of here. I want to go home, and I'll tell you everything I know."

"Deal," Jake said, knowing he would have helped the young woman regardless. He handed her the bill.

"Her uncle just left with her."

"You little bitch," Mrs. Leake said, running down the stairs.

Jake stepped in front of the madame and grinned. "You lost."

The woman growled. "Not necessarily. Not yet."

"Mack, take the girl upstairs and help her pack her things."

"Nothing to pack. Just put me on a stage back home."

"Honey, you can't travel wearing your undergarments," Mack said. "Come on, we'll find you a dress. But we gotta hurry."

"Don't come back."

The kid smiled. "Never planned on it."

Mack pushed Mrs. Leake out of the way and they ran up the stairs. In fewer than five minutes, they returned.

"After this is over, I'm coming back for you," Jake warned the madam. "You just crossed the line when you helped kidnap my wife."

"I didn't kidnap her," she said and he feared she was trying to stall them.

"You aided and helped hide her. I'll be back. Hope you like jail. We'll talk soon," he promised as he held the door open and they hurried out.

Once they were outside, he turned to the young girl. "Do you have any idea where her uncle took her?"

"No, but she was out. He had to carry her down the stairs."

Anger rode Jake hard as he gazed at the young girl. "The money should get you to where you're going and also be enough for food. Be careful. Don't trust anyone."

Tears gathered in her eyes and she reached up and hugged him. "Thank you. I'm going home."

She quickly hugged Mack and then she ran down the street toward the stage office.

"The stage is coming in today," Mack said. "Look, there's a notice up on the board. It was running late when we were there earlier."

If her uncle was the masked bandit, then he would want to rob the stage today. Yet, he'd been seen carrying Anna out of the brothel. Would he take Anna to the robbery? Especially if he planned on killing her anyway?

"Do you think he's going to miss robbing the stage to kill Anna?"

Mack's brows drew together in a frown. "No, but he might kill her at the robbery."

"That's what I'm thinking. Let's go," Jake said. "We have a robbery to intercept."

CHAPTER 16

"*N*o," Anna said fear clutching her heart. "I'm not robbing the stage for you."

Leaning against a tree, her uncle pulled out his Colt 45, aimed it at her and pulled back the hammer. "Then I'll shoot you right here. Your father refused to help us after he learned what I was doing, so I ambushed him and your mother."

Rage like a storming wildfire consumed Anna. "You shot and killed your own sister? What a cold-hearted bastard you are."

"What was I supposed to do? Let her run to the Texas Rangers and tell them her brother was going to rob the stage, to steal enough money to go gold hunting? All her life, she had it easy while I had to grovel to get a job with my brother-in-law."

Anna remembered hearing her parents arguing about her uncle. Her father had called him lazy and now she understood why he wanted the gold. He didn't want to work for a living. He wanted to steal from others, so he didn't have to work. Now that she thought about it, the work around the ranch had not been the same, since her father passed away.

"I'm not robbing the stage," she said again with force. "You just want to kill me in the process and then everyone will think that I was the masked bandit while you and your cohorts leave town."

Her heart was skipping in her chest. If her uncle didn't kill her, the shotgun rider would. It was a devious plan, and it could very well work.

A cold maniacal laughter came from him. "No one said you were stupid."

The more she thought about this, the more a plan came together in her head. What if she just rode off in the other direction as fast as she could. "I'll be on a horse?"

"Yes," he said.

"What about a gun?"

"Sure, but there will be no bullets. All you have to do is make the robbery a success."

This robbery would never be a success. This robbery was sacrificing her life and letting her be accused of being the masked bandit, so he could ride away.

"And what? You're going to let me go?"

"No," he said.

"Where are you going to be?"

"Right back here in the woods, watching and making sure it goes according to plan," he said with a smile.

"So you can shoot me in the back?"

"Now, would I do that to my niece?"

Of course, he would. Who was he kidding?

"You killed your sister," she replied, knowing full well

that's what he meant to do. She gazed around the country-side and knew she had very little choice but hoped her men would soon rescue her or she would die alone.

All she wanted was one more chance to gaze into their eyes, feel their muscular bodies, and experience their love-making once again.

Tears filled her eyes. She loved them with all her heart and had since they asked to marry her. She even loved their weird ideas of love of being with two men and couldn't imagine her life any other way, because she could never choose between them. They were her men. Her lovers. Her husbands.

"Get a move on. The stage should be arriving in the next ten minutes if it's on time. Here, put this pants and shirt on along with the mask."

He tossed her the clothes and she stared at them, hating what he was doing to her.

"Get them on. If you don't put them on, I'll strip you naked right here and put them on you myself," he screamed.

"Turn your back," she said.

"No, you're not getting away. Now put the damn clothes on."

She had no pantaloons on beneath her dress. Nothing as she slowly unbuttoned the dress, hoping her men would magically appear. But they didn't.

Suddenly the idea of slipping the pants on under her dress occurred to her and once they were on, she pulled the gift from her men off and hung it up in the tree. Maybe they would find it there. It was her favorite dress of all time.

Thank goodness she had been able to purchase some undergarments the last time she visited the mercantile. With only her chemise on, she hurriedly put the man's shirt on. The clothes were baggy on her, but maybe that would help them to recognize she wasn't the real bandit.

When she turned to face him, he laughed and handed her the bandit's mask.

"Slip it on. And then get on your horse. Here is your gun. Don't worry, I took out the bullets. Your job is to stop the stagecoach. I'll do the rest."

"Like kill me," she said. "I hope you burn in hell for what you've done to our family."

He grinned. "Keep the fires burning for me."

"Fuck you," she said and climbed on the horse.

"I hear the stagecoach coming. Get ready."

Tears filled her eyes; she was going to die. The images of her husbands came to mind and she urged the horse forward. If she died, she wanted her last thoughts to be of the men she loved with all her heart.

CHAPTER 17

$\mathcal{M}$ack and Jake pushed their horses as fast as they dared to reach the stagecoach. Since they had no idea where the robberies occurred, they were just rushing on the road to intercept the stage.

As they passed trees and brush and cacti, Mack wondered if the bandit was hiding behind the foliage.

"There," Jake cried.

The coach was coming around a corner hurrying toward the town of Blessing. Pulling back on their horses, they waited to meet them on the road, when suddenly the masked bandit rode out from the woods.

"Stop," the voice yelled. It was not a manly voice, but rather high pitched. Either the masked bandit was a woman or a man whose voice sounded like a woman.

The shotgun who sat on the box, rose and pointed his weapon at the horseback rider.

"Stop," the masked bandit yelled and pointed his weapon in a way that Mack had never seen before. It was limp not rigid like he would be using it to shoot anyone. If fired, it would fall from his hand and then it hit Mack.

Dark hair tumbled down in the back of her hat and he knew.

He recognized that neck and the hands and arms of the person robbing the Concord Coach. He'd kissed her and fucked her and his heart belonged to her.

Spurring his horse, he rode as fast as he could toward the masked bandit. Jake did as well. When they were near. Jake pulled out his badge.

"Texas Rangers," he called.

Mack leaped from his horse onto the back of the masked bandit, pulling her soft body against his just as a gunshot rang out from behind them, twisting her until they fell from the horse onto the hard ground.

His breath left his body at the impact as he rolled Anna to protect her from the fall. Damn, he was getting too old for this.

A burning sensation of pure fire trailed up his arm to his shoulder.

"Stop him. He's getting away," Anna cried.

"Who?"

"My uncle Walter," she cried. "I'm not the masked bandit. He made me do this, so he could kill me and make it look like I was the robber."

Jake spurred his horse and took off after Walter.

"Are you hurt?" Mack said with a groan.

"No, but you're bleeding," she said as she rolled him to his side to see where he was bleeding.

"Thank God," she said. "It's only a scratch."

The stagecoach had pulled to a stop and the man

holding the shotgun came over to her. Mack could see he was not certain of what was going on.

"I don't know who you are, young lady, but you're not the same person who has been robbing this coach," he said. "Are you another robber?"

With a laugh, she hung her head. "No, the real robber was trying to make it appear that I was the bandit, so he could kill me and everyone would think I'd done it. You can check my gun. It's empty."

The man picked up her Colt, pulled back the revolver and saw the empty chamber. "You're right. You don't have a bullet in the chamber."

It was a genius plan that either the Shotgun rider or her uncle would have shot and killed her, thinking they had thwarted yet another robbery. But did this mean they were no longer going to rob the stage?

Mack pulled Anna to him, thinking of how close to losing her they had come. If Jake didn't catch that son of a bitch, then he would and the bastard wouldn't live to see another day.

"I'm sorry," Anna said. "I didn't want to stop you, but it was that or my life."

"Lady, you don't make a very good robber," he said with a smile. "I kept thinking this bandit is sure not very persuasive. In the past, they pointed their gun at us and fired to make us pull over."

The passengers were getting out of the stagecoach and walking around. They came over to Mack and Anna.

"Young woman, you should be ashamed of yourself," one older woman said.

"It was rob the stage or my life," she said. "Instead Mack saved me and took the bullet."

All Mack wanted to do was hold onto Anna and instead there were people everywhere circling the stagecoach.

The older woman gasped when she saw the blood trickling down the back of his arm. "Put him in the stage and let's take him to the doctor."

"Thanks, ma'am, but my partner should be back soon and I'm hoping he will have the real masked bandit."

The old lady nodded. "Thank you, Mr. Ranger."

Mack smiled. It was nice when people said thank you, but it was odd that she had no sympathy for Anna.

"I think we should get you to a doctor," Anna said.

"No, we're waiting on Jake."

She bit her lip, and it was all Mack could do not to reach out, to pull her to him and kiss her like he wanted to in front of all these people.

"Anna, you—"

Gunshots rang out and Mack pulled Anna down and rolled over her, covering her body with his.

The passengers scrambled for cover, some even crawling back inside the stagecoach.

Walter Farris rode his horse back into their area, his eyes were glazed with shock as he raised his pistol to fire at Mack who had Anna beneath him.

"You little bitch," he said, raising his gun.

Jake fired a shot, killing the man instantly.

People screamed as the man fell to the ground. Mack wasn't certain of how Anna would react as he rolled off her. There was her guardian, her uncle, the man she had depended on, lying in the dirt, dead.

She rose, hugged Mack and said, "Thank God, he's dead. Now we need to catch the banker and Mrs. Leake. She's part of this. The banker and her are running off to Mexico to live on the beach."

Mack and Jake smiled. It seemed that their woman had been doing some investigating on her own.

$\mathcal{S}$omehow they had to catch the banker and his whore red handed or it could be hard to prove that both were involved. After all, the banker was a fine upstanding citizen in the community with a wife and two kids.

And Anna, not having the best reputation, claimed that he was having an affair with the madame of the whorehouse. Who would believe them? They placed Walter on his horse and tied him the best they could to appear he was riding between them into town. Like they were taking him to the jail.

They needed the citizens to believe he was alive.

Jake hoped that somehow Mrs. Leake and George Elam would believe that Walter was sitting in jail spilling his guts to the sheriff. While he and Mack sought out the two of them and somehow wrangled a confession from each.

"Can I go with you?" Anna asked.

"No, we're going to leave you with the sheriff."

His heart had almost come out of his chest when he

realized that she was being the bandit and robbing the stage. A poor one at that, but still the shotgun didn't know she wasn't the real bandit.

He needed to know she was safe.

"I don't want to stay with the sheriff," she said.

Jake gave her a warning glance. She knew the consequences for not obeying. And after today, they had enough excitement trying to keep her safe. She had come so close to being shot. He'd even thought of shooting the masked bandit himself.

Until Mack recognized their wife.

"You are to stay with the sheriff until we come get you," Mack said.

"Even with a dead body there?"

"Even with a dead body," Jake said, knowing that this woman could get into more trouble in just a matter of moments. "By the way, you did an excellent job defending yourself and I loved your clue."

She smiled. "Thank you. But I could help you convince them to talk."

"No," both men said at the same time, which made her jump.

"All right. I guess I'm staying at the sheriff's."

They pulled up in front of the sheriff's and both men helped Walter off his horse. Already his body was beginning to cool and if they had waited much longer, they would not have been able to do this.

The three of them walked in and sat the body in one of the chairs.

"What the hell?"

Mack told Sheriff Ingram about what had happened

and how they killed the masked bandit, but that the banker and Mrs. Leake were involved.

The sheriff shook his head. "I'm not surprised. How can I help you?"

"Keep the body here and Anna. She's given us enough excitement for one day."

"All right. I'll keep her safe. Good luck getting confessions from the other two."

Jake and Mack walked out the door, leaving Anna in the hands of the sheriff. First, they went to the bordello, which Jake was sick of being inside. When they walked in, the place went quiet.

"Where's Mrs. Leake?"

"Gone. She left not long after you. Packed her bags and hit the road."

He felt skeptical.

"And you're telling me the truth?"

"Yes, we're talking about what to do if the bordello closes. She's not here. You can check if you want to, but she's gone," a woman told him.

Without a word, they hurried out the door. If they didn't find them, then they would return, but he probably scared her enough that she left.

Next, they went to the banker's house and when his wife answered the door, Jake felt bad for the woman. She had done nothing wrong and yet her husband would soon make a wreck of their home.

"I'm sorry, he's not come home. Earlier I went to the bank, but he wasn't there either."

"Thanks, ma'am," they said and walked away not telling

her why they were searching for him. Why destroy the woman's world just yet?

As they hurried down the steps, Mack looked at Jake. "They've gone after the gold. He and Mrs. Leake are getting ready to head out of town."

"You're right," Jake said. "Let's go get them."

They rode out to the ranch, but the place was dark. No activity, nothing. It was deserted. They peeked in the windows and walked around the place. Empty.

As they were walking back to their horses. Jake shook his head, his mind swirling with questions.

"Do you think they're gone?"

"I don't know. I'm confused. The gold was in the safe at Anna's house. The safe was still there, but was the gold?"

"Let's collect our bride and call it a night. It's getting late. We'll start again in the morning."

"Sounds good. I can't wait to get her home and hold her and fuck her," Mack said.

"You're wounded. You can't have sex tonight," Jake said, grinning as the sun slid down below the horizon, casting the earth in dusk.

"The hell I can't. Unless I'm dying, I'm still up to fucking our sweet bride."

As they rode into town, they noticed it seemed quieter than normal. Like everyone had disappeared off the streets.

They hitched their horses outside the sheriff's office and when they walked in, no one was there. Not the sheriff or Anna.

A shout came from the street and they rushed outside to see what was going on.

The banker's wife, Katherine, stood in the street with her shotgun raised.

"If you want to leave me, that's fine. You're a lousy husband anyway. But you're not leaving with that whore," she said.

A crowd of spectators was standing around them.

"Katherine, put the gun down. You don't know what you're doing," the banker said. "You're going to get me in all kinds of trouble."

She laughed. "Yes, I do know what I'm doing. I'm stopping you from leaving with the madam of the whore house you own. You don't think I know, but I do. I learned last year that you owned the whorehouse and I thought why? Now I know."

The madam stood and the woman turned her gun toward her. "Don't move or I will take great pleasure in shooting you. My kids are not going to have a father because of you."

Mrs. Leake slowly sank down on the wagon seat.

"I've hated you for a long time and want to kill you, but then our children would not have a parent. So instead, we wait for the rangers."

Anna stood in the back of the crowd and Jake was filled with relief to know that she was not somehow involved in this little theater. But it did help him with his plan to arrest the banker and Mrs. Leake.

Walking through the crowd, he came to the scene. "Good evening, Katherine. Good to see you again."

She gave him a glance, but kept her eyes trained on her husband and his mistress. "Anna said you would come. But what can you do?"

"I'm here to arrest your husband and Mrs. Leake. In the back of that wagon is the missing gold. Walter Farris, George Elam, and Mrs. Leake have been stealing the shipments from the stagecoach. Only Walter is dead."

A gasp came from the crowd.

Mack walked to the back of the wagon.

The banker wiped the sweat from his brow, though the evening was chilly. "Stop. You won't find anything back there but our suitcases. This is between me and my wife."

Mack started to laugh. "Oh, I didn't know you could wear gold. I see at least eight boxes marked *gold*."

Jake knew an emotional spouse was capable of many things. "Mrs. Elam, please put the gun down. I'll take it from here."

She gazed up her husband, tears filling her eyes. "You're nothing more than a thief and a whoremonger. Rot in hell."

The gun slid to the ground and Anna came to her side. "It's all right, Mrs. Elam. You and the children are safe."

For once, Jake was glad that Anna interfered and moved Mrs. Elam out of harm's way. "Step down out of the wagon. George Elam and Josephine Leake, you're under arrest for robbery."

Both of them surrendered and Mack and Jake slapped the handcuffs on them. The sheriff walked up and shook his head.

"You're going to enjoy the hospitality in my jail. Until we have a hearing. Let's see, hanging is a possibility."

Mrs. Elam watched as her husband and his mistress walked to the jail, hands restrained.

Anna came to Jake's side. "I feel so sorry for her."

"Me too," he said.

Katherine Elam stood off to the side, gazing at the man she was married to.

"Are you going to be all right?" Jake asked the new single parent.

"Yes," she whispered. "I never knew he was capable."

She turned to Anna. "Thank you for coming to me tonight and telling me. I'm sorry I didn't believe you at first."

A rush of anger filled Jake. The woman had left the jail and put herself in danger. How had she gotten away from Seth? Of course, she probably snuck out.

Anna gave him a quick glance. "It's all right. I'm just sorry it turned out this way."

Mack took Anna by the arm. "Good night, Mrs. Elam."

"Good night," she said as they marched Anna to their horses.

"You're in trouble," Jake said.

She sighed. "I know, but it was worth it. We caught them. I was afraid you were not going to arrive in time to arrest him."

Jake shook his head. Anna was the most stubborn woman ever. And tonight, she would be punished.

CHAPTER 19

*A*nna knew she was in trouble but she didn't care. Disobeying had been worth it, and she didn't think she had been in danger. A wife deserved to know what her husband was doing and if she had been in Katherine's shoes, she would have wanted to know what the father of her children was planning.

When they arrived at the house, Jake lifted her from Mack's horse. "In the house. Remove your clothes and wait for us, face down on the bed, with your ass lifted."

"Because of me, we captured them," she said, not really defending herself, but wanting him to be aware that without her help, they would still be searching for the banker and he might even have gotten away.

"Doesn't matter. You disobeyed," Mack said, turning his horse toward the barn.

"Get in the house," Jake said.

Anna whirled on her heels and walked into the house and went into the bedroom. It wasn't fair. Yes, she had disobeyed, but it was for a good reason. One she thought they should overlook punishing her for.

And while she did enjoy being spanked for pleasure, she had received one of Jake's spankings for disobeying and he deliberately made it sting, so she would not disobey again.

With a sigh, she removed her clothes and lay on the bed as she was told. At the last moment, she grabbed a pillow and took Jake's belt and strapped it around her buttocks.

Now he could spank her and she wouldn't feel a thing.

Fifteen minutes later, she heard her men quietly talking as they entered the bedroom. They went silent and oh how she wished she could peek and see their faces, but she knew better than to sneak a glimpse of them.

"Anna, you continue to try me," Jake said as he removed his clothes.

"Honey, we were only going to give you ten licks, but you just got an additional five. Now take the pillow off," Mack said, yanking off his shirt and pants

Turning over, she gave them a defiant look. Their large cocks swollen and ready. "I just thought if you were going to spank me for something I didn't deserve punishment for, then I should have an advantage."

Jake took her by the arm and pulled her onto his lap. His huge cock slid up between her legs. "If you didn't disobey us so much, you probably would have gotten away with this one time. But I don't think you realize that when we say obey us, we mean it. You're like a naughty child always getting into trouble."

Anna sighed. "All right, get it over with."

"Oh no," Mack said. "That's not how this is going to work this time."

He moved in closer, his cock almost at the same level as her mouth.

She glanced at him, and for a second, she didn't know what he intended and then he pulled her to him, his lips covering hers. It was so strange how both men were different. Mack kissed like Satan, his mouth all but consuming her. The way his tongue swept into her mouth commanding her surrender, creating a moan from deep inside her. It was like his kiss seemed to connect all her body parts from deep in her cunny to her mouth.

Like flint to tender, she could feel her body begin to heat. A growing sense of surrender overcame her. She wanted both of her men. And she knew they had both claimed her heart.

And then Jake's hand slid down her waist to the center of her body. His fingers slid over her flesh stroking her creating a storm of feelings. An urgency filled her and she knew she wanted their cocks to fill her. To soothe the overwhelming need consuming her.

Mack released her lips and she gasped. "Please, Jake fuck me."

"No," he said as his finger begin once again to twist and tweak the little nub between her legs.

"Oh, Mack please," she cried as he reached for her nipples, pulling and twisting them, sending pulsating waves through her.

"No," he said. "And don't you dare come or you're going to get twenty licks."

Her heart raced and she could feel her orgasm rushing at her and she wanted to come so badly but knew they would refuse her.

"I can't stop it. I'm going to come," she cried.

They both released her, leaving her in swirling mass of confusion and desire gripping her, strangling her with need.

"Are you ready to receive your punishment?" Jake asked her, his hand gliding over her buttock.

"Just do it," she cried. "Get it over with."

"No, you're not ready," Jake said as his finger swirled around her backside and she gasped as the heat once again sent her to the edge.

"Why are you doing this?"

"We want you to understand why it's important that you obey us. You are our life now and the fear of losing you is terrifying," Jake said as his fingers delved inside her, causing her to moan.

"We will keep you in a constant state of need until you're ready to surrender," Mack said. "Surrender to us and obey our every command."

Anna gasped as pleasure took her right up to the edge, and once again, they stopped. She wanted to scream with frustration but knew that would only prolong her torment. Twice more they took her to the edge and then backed away leaving her gasping with need, her pussy throbbing, her breasts aching and her breathing harsh sounding to her ears.

Couldn't they see what they were doing to her? Finally, the realization that the torture they were inflicting was worse than the punishment reached her dulled mind.

"All right, I surrender. Punish me," she gasped, knowing she couldn't hold out much longer.

Mack took her by the hand and laid her over his naked

lap. "I'm going to give you seven licks and then Jake is going to give you eight. Don't fight me or you'll receive even more."

A whimper escaped from her and she took a deep breath, just before she felt the palm of his hand hit her buttocks. The first one stung, but what was worse, was the way his fingers seemed to delve between her legs and find her clit.

"Count with me," he said.

"One," she said, her voice breathless from the way his fingers made her feel.

Once again, his palm connected with her buttocks, but this time, the blow landed more between her legs, causing her cunt to vibrate, sending both pain and need aching through her.

"Two," she said, knowing she would be a mess once this was over.

On and on, the blows seemed to rain down on her ass and even her pussy until finally she was sobbing, her buttocks were burning and she still had seven more to go.

"Eight," she cried as tears flowed into her hair that swung to the floor.

Mack helped her stand and then they laid her across Jake's lap. The last spanking she received from him, hurt even worse than Mack's.

"Anna, my father use to say it hurt him more than it did me when he gave me a spanking. I now understand his reasoning. But still you must learn to obey us for your own safety," Jake said, his hand massaging the burning in her cheeks.

All she could do was lay there, wishing his fingers

would bring this torment to an end. That they would make her come and end the need raging inside her. That they would only give her a pleasure filled spanking and not this transgression one.

And yet, she understood what they were doing and why. But that didn't mean she had to like it.

Smack! His hand landed on her buttocks and she jerked from the force. Tears ran down her cheeks.

Smack! He hit her again and yet this time, it didn't feel as hard and his fingers stroked her clit.

Smack! And she began to sob. "Jake, please."

"Are you going to obey us?"

"Yes," she said, knowing right now she would agree to anything.

"If you don't, your punishment will be even more severe next time."

He pulled her up in his arms and held her close as she cried, his lips kissing her along her forehead, her cheek and down her face.

"Remember how I told you that I had a sister?"

With a sniff, she said, "Yes."

"She was kidnapped by a woman who had a brothel. They sold her virginity and made her into a whore. By the time I found her, she was dead. She lasted one year before she killed herself. When we came home and found you had been taken, I was terrified the same thing had happened to you. I was so afraid we had lost you forever."

Her life and his sister's were almost parallel, because she had been sold to the brothel. But someone helped her escape and he would be forever grateful to that person, whoever they were. Now she had no idea who that person was, but if she ever learned who it was, she would thank them.

"But you found me. I knew you would," she said. "I trusted that my two strong rangers would find me."

Mack wrapped an arm around her.

"With you, we want a family, a home and we will protect you with our lives. Don't make it harder for us to keep you safe," Mack said. "I'm anxiously awaiting the day we have our first child. I miss my family so much, but with you, we have a chance to create the home I miss."

Warmth spread through her chest. She loved these men. They were her husbands, and she didn't care what anyone else thought, they were hers until death parted them.

Jake pulled her back and stared into her eyes. "We will protect you with our life, but you need to know that we will always have your best interest at heart. So when we tell you no, there's a reason. What if tonight, George Elam and Mrs. Leake had caught you going to his home? What do you think they would have done to you?"

"Kill me," she said softly.

"That's right. Let us be your protectors," he said.

Stunned that these two men, her husbands, were so worried about her safety, her protection, she reached out and grabbed Mack's hand as she leaned against Jake's chest. "You both are my everything. And now hopefully, we can begin our lives without fear."

Jake leaned back on the bed and pulled her with him. "Now we're going to fuck you."

"But first it's time for another butt plug. You should be getting close to us both being able to take you at the same time."

Anna gazed as Mack went to the dresser and pulled out a larger one. Jake moved her until she was lying on top of him.

"On your knees," he said as she rose over him.

Mack came behind her and put his fingers into her dripping cunny and took the excess moisture and lathered up the butt plug.

Jake placed his fingers on her chin and turned her mouth until he could consume her lips. His lips ravaged hers as he controlled the kiss, gripping her cheeks with one hand while his mouth devoured hers. All the feelings from before rushed through her as he kissed her.

His kiss was much more urgent and demanding than Mack's. It had strength and power and commanded that she succumb to him. And she gladly gave him her all.

With a whimper, she felt Mack's hand caressing her backside, rubbing her, soothing her and then his fingers probed her ass, stroking her before she felt his digit sinking into her, preparing her, stretching her.

But Jake demanded her attention, his lips ravished her mouth, his tongue commanded attention.

He broke the kiss and she gasped for breath. "Look at me, Anna. I want to see the passion explode inside you when Mack puts the butt plug in."

A groan came from her when she felt the butt plug slowly being pushed inside her. While it wasn't painful, it left her feeling full in her backside and she longed for Mack or Jake's cock to fill her.

Mack's fingers stroked her clit and she moaned, not from the pressure but from the need to be filled with cock.

"Oh, Mack," she cried, her eyes closing.

"Look at me," Jake told her, his fingers reaching down and twisting her nipples.

"Aargh," she cried. "Please do something. I need you."

She felt Mack thump the butt plug sending a shimmer of heat through her. Then he pulled it out, twisted it and shoved it back in.

"That's how it's going to feel when we both fuck you," Mack said.

"Please," she cried.

Jake slid down until his cock was at the entrance to her pussy. With a quick shove, he pushed his way inside and she screamed at the feeling that overwhelmed her.

"Jake," she cried as he began to stroke her, his dick hitting the wall of her womb, her inside muscles clenching him as he fucked her. While he gave her his cock, Mack twisted and pulled the butt plug. She was filled to the brim and all she could do was hang on to her men.

Staring into Jake's eyes, she saw them darken with heat. "I love how your cock feels inside me. I love the way it brings me so much pleasure."

His eyes widened and she knew her words had pushed him to the edge.

"Come for me, now," he cried.

And she did. Finally, the release she'd been seeking exploded through her and she screamed as her body seemed to set sail in the wind and carry her to unknown heights before she came crashing back down to earth. Back into the arms of her men who protected her.

"Oh, Jake," she said with a whimper collapsing on top of him.

"Not yet," he said. "On your hands and knees. Mack

wants you to fuck him. Then I want you to watch me while he fucks you."

She glanced behind her and smiled, knowing she always enjoyed the way he made her climax.

"Up on your knees," he commanded giving her pussy a sharp slap.

It was a wake-up call. A demand from her to give him attention. She slowly got up on her knees and then he slapped her pussy again.

A moan came from her not of pain, but pure pleasure.

"You're ours," he said.

"Tell me who you belong to," he demanded.

"I'm your and Jake's wife," she said, looking back over her shoulder at him. "All yours. Now please fuck me, the way only you can."

A smile spread across his face, but he shook his head. "No, I've changed my mind. Roll over on your back. I want you to see my cock slamming into your pussy."

She rolled over onto her back and Mack lifted her legs and handed them to Jake. Then he lifted her hips to meet his cock.

He spread her vulva with his fingers and grinned. "You have the sweetest little pussy and I'm going to conquer it."

He slammed his cock into her pussy and she groaned at the tremors that rocked through. She gazed at him through half slitted lids watching his cock go in and out, pounding into her.

"Mack, I can't wait for you to both take me," she moaned knowing the words were true. The thought of them both at the same time had her breathing fast and loud. Both of them taking her, commanding and doing whatever they wanted to do at their will. She was completely at their mercy and she loved it.

With his fingers, he reached back and thumped the butt plug sending shivers through her, spiraling her closer and closer to the edge.

"Fuck me, Mack. Fuck me," she screamed, knowing she only needed that release that had been denied her earlier. Knowing that not one man, but both of them, were the only ones who could give her the relief she sought.

"Squeeze me," he groaned.

And she did, clenching her muscles, surrounding his cock, knowing that soon he would coat the walls of her pussy with his seed. Wanting it and him.

"Come for me, now," he said with a groan as he held her pussy up against him as she undulated around his cock.

"Mack," she screamed as she fell back to earth, shattered.

The feel of his seed filled her and she knew that her life would never be the same. These were her men. Her lovers and they controlled her in every way.

Exhausted, Mack let her body slide down to the bed and then he crawled in beside her. In between her men, her eyes closed and with a sigh, she thought she couldn't wait to do this again. And again.

CHAPTER 20

*A*nna walked through the mercantile with her shopping basket looking for just a few items for her husbands. It was Christmas Eve and tonight they planned on going to church and then coming home and opening presents.

With her uncle dead, the ranch was once again hers and she had made plans that she hoped her men would approve of. Though they didn't like it when she went into town alone, she had managed to be accompanied to the lawyer's office where she asked them to wait outside.

They weren't too happy, but how could she make this a surprise if they came in with her.

Today, she just needed some little things. A new shaving mug for Mack. A new tie to wear to church for Jake. Nothing much, but just a little something for their first Christmas together.

"Son," a female said, "I told you we're not going to have much of a Christmas since I lost my job."

The voice sent a chill down her spine. She knew that

voice. She recognized it.

Turning, she walked toward a lady with a big strapping teenage son. Tears swelled in her eyes.

The woman stopped and stared when she approached her.

"Thank you," she gasped as tears rolled down her cheeks. "Thank you for dropping me on the ranger's doorstep that night. I don't know why you did it, but from the bottom of my heart thank you."

The woman smiled. "I wasn't certain that you wouldn't have me arrested."

"How did you know they were rangers?"

"My son saw them take off their badges before they rode into town. He told me that two rangers had moved into that house."

"You saved me from a terrible life. And now, I'm married to one of the rangers. But why would you do such a thing?"

The woman sighed, her head dropped and her eyes filled with tears. "I had a daughter once. She was kidnapped and forced to work in a brothel. Since, my husband's death, I worked in the kitchen at the brothel and every chance I got, I saved one of you girls from that terrible life. Wishing that someone would have saved my daughter."

Anna wrapped her arms around the woman and hugged her close. "Thank you. I know I probably gave you trouble that night, but I was so afraid."

The woman hugged her and laughed. "Yes, you were a handful. But I'm so glad we saved you."

Anna leaned back. "What are you going to do now that

the brothel has closed."

"I don't know. We grew accustomed to the money and I really want my son, Mike, to go to college."

The idea came to her suddenly and yet she knew better than to offer something without talking to her husbands. But if they took her up on her offer of being partners at the Riverbend Ranch, then it would be good if they could hire a cook.

"I may have a job for you, but I can't talk about it now. After Christmas, I'll let you know."

The woman's eyes brightened and she smiled. "That would be wonderful."

"In the meantime, I want you have to a wonderful Christmas."

She turned and glanced at the boy. "Pick out something for Christmas. And," she hollered to Mr. Bailey, owner of the mercantile, "put a ham on my bill for Mrs. ..."

The woman smiled. "Mrs. Roberts. Clara Roberts. But you don't have to do this. Saving you is all we need."

Anna hugged her again. "No, it's my honor. Please, my Christmas gift to you."

"Thank you," Clara said.

Just then Jake and Mack peeked inside the store and motioned for her to hurry.

"I've got to go, Clara, but I hope you and your son have the best Christmas ever."

"Thank you," the woman said.

Anna hurried up to the counter and put her purchases and those for Clara and her son on the Riverbend Ranch account. After all, the ranch was hers and she hoped to be living there again soon.

CHAPTER 21

*J*ake glanced at his wife and thought she had never looked more beautiful. She had come out of the mercantile this afternoon, happily chattering about she had just met the woman who saved her. It seemed the cook at the brothel had stolen her out from under Mrs. Leake's nose and dropped her off at their address because they were rangers and she thought they could save Anna.

As soon as Christmas was over, Jake wanted to drop by and thank the woman for delivering his wife to his doorstep. It was the best Christmas present ever.

It had been a full evening with them attending church and then coming home to fresh apple pie. Now they were opening Christmas gifts.

"Your turn," Anna said. "But I want you both to open it at the same time."

They each had been given a small box and an envelope. Jake felt certain he knew what was in the box and it made him happy. But the envelope, he had no clue.

His wife was one for surprises.

"Open the envelope first," she instructed.

They glanced at one another and Jake drew out a letter. Mack had one exactly like it. For a moment, he felt fear that she was saying goodbye, but then shock overcame him at the generosity.

"If we're going to have a family, I really don't want my men gone all the time. I want you with me watching our children grow, helping with their care and molding of their personalities. It takes both a mother and fathers and that's what I want for our children. You are husbands and you should be my partners."

The letter was written by a solicitor giving them each a third of the property if they wanted to become her partner. His chest contracted at what she was offering them. But he couldn't take it.

Mack glanced at Jake and smiled. "Since we married, I've been wondering how in the world I could go off and leave you. I'm agreeable as long as our children inherit the land once we're gone."

That was a great idea.

"Absolutely," she said smiling at him. "But I wanted it be our partnership, not just my land."

Jake frowned and she could tell he wasn't as certain as Mack. "This is your family inheritance. I don't want to take it from you."

"You're not. As my partners I expect you to make the ranch profitable again. The books are in a mess and it looks like we're losing money. You will raise cattle, horses, sheep, whatever to get it going once again. I'm going to be raising our family. Your job as partner is to make the ranch into a thriving business to give to our children. And believe me, you will have your work cut out for you."

A grin spread across his face. "But why not just give it to our children?"

"Because I love you and Mack with all my heart. I trust you and expect you to show our children how a partnership made our ranch into a family dynasty. I can't do that alone and need your help. All you have to do is sign the papers and you're a partner."

How could he deny her? How could he tell her this was his dream. A ranch with a houseful of children.

With a sigh, Jake smiled. "Well, when you put it that way. Anna Best Nash, you have owned my heart since the day I opened that door and found you in a potato sack."

She grinned and threw her arms around him and kissed him. "I'm yours and Mack's."

Mack slid his arms around the back of her and she leaned her head back and reached up and kissed him.

"Now open the box," she said.

They broke apart and when they opened the box, there were gold bands inside. Each man had his own wedding band with a message on the inside that said, "I'm yours."

"I'm your woman and you're my men."

"God, I love you, Anna," Mack said.

"Well, if you love me, then it's time you showed me," she said, standing and running into the bedroom. "Someone needs to fuck me."

The two men glanced at one another and then they were removing their clothes, dropping them onto the floor as they hurried into the bedroom.

She lay on the bed, head down on the bed and her ass sticking up in the air.

"Would you look at that sight," Mack said. "I think tonight is the night that we both claim her. Make her ours in every possible way."

Jake's heart slammed into his chest. This was the best Christmas ever. Never would he have dreamed that he would have a wife so beautiful and be part owner in a ranch. And yet he felt grateful and so much in love.

"Let's flip a coin to see who gets her ass," Mack said with a grin.

"No, you took her maidenhead, so I get her ass first," Jake replied.

Mack went to her head and lifted her. "Tonight, we're going to take you at the same time. But I promise it will be good."

Anna smiled. "I trust you."

"Oh, yes, honey," Jake said at her backside. "I promise you, we're going to make it very good for you."

Jake put his fingers on the butt plug and slowly pulled it and then pushed it back in, twisting and churning it inside her back passage.

Soft moans came from her and he knew she was enjoying what he was doing.

With his other hand, he reached between her legs and tweaked her clit and she pushed her backside back toward him. The honey of her arousal coated his fingers and he pulled the butt plug from her and then dipped his fingers into her ass.

"Jake," she cried.

With a nod to Mack, he moved beneath her and put his cock at the entrance to her pussy.

"First, I'm going in and then Jake. We'll take it slow," he assured her. "Don't close your eyes. Look at me. Let me see the passion building in your gaze. The hunger filling you."

Anna moaned and he shoved his cock into her willing cunny.

"Mack," she moaned.

Unable to resist, Jake slapped her ass and she squealed.

"Your ass is so beautiful," Jake said. "It's hard not to turn it pink."

He reached down and kissed her on her butt cheeks and then he bit her.

"Jake," she groaned.

Crawling up on the bed, he placed his cock at her back entrance and slowly begin to push inside her.

"Relax, Anna and let me in. I promise to make you feel good. Let your husbands give you pleasure."

The words had her breathing heavily and suddenly he was inside her and she clenched his cock with her ass muscles. It was such an amazing feeling that he had to stop himself from spilling his seed right then.

"Honey, you do that much more and I'm not going to last long," he groaned.

Soon, he and Mack had a rhythm going—in and out, and each time she would squeeze his cock. Already he could feel his seed churning inside him, ready to explode.

Knowing that he wasn't going to last long and wanting her to come with him, he reached down and slapped her ass again.

"Jake, I'm going to come," she cried. "Mack, help me."

"Go ahead, sweetheart," Mack said.

Rocking her between them, Jake shoved his cock as far as he could into her ass, his seed exploding from him coating the inside of her rectum. With a groan, he tried to make his orgasm last as long as possible.

Mack jerked her to him as she screamed her release.

"Oh, oh, oh, my," she cried as Jake slumped on top of her holding her as close to his heart as he could. This was his wife. His woman. His and Mack's forever woman.

Mack pulled from her and the two men put her between them, holding her in their arms.

"Best Christmas ever," she said with a sigh.

"Agree," Mack said.

"Our first Christmas together. I love you, Anna," Jake said.

"I love you," Mack repeated.

"And I love you, my Christmas cowboys," Anna said, a satisfied smile on her face.

CHAPTER 22

*N*ine months later, Mack and Jake paced the living room in the ranch home. They had moved here in January and since that time, the two had quit the Texas Rangers and now were ranchers. Their first cattle drive was behind them, and so far, it seemed they had a successful season.

Mrs. Clara Roberts was their new housekeeper and cook. She came running down the stairs. "It won't be long now. The midwife said to tell you, if you want to see the birth or cut the umbilical cord to come now."

They both raced up the stairs past Mrs. Roberts and into the bedroom they all shared.

Anna lay on the bed, panting. The midwife glanced up at them. "Gentlemen, one more push and your son or daughter will be born."

"If either one of you fucks me again and gets me pregnant, you're dead men."

"Now, Anna, once you see this beautiful babe, you'll soon be wanting another," the midwife said with a chuckle.

"Let them have the next one then," she said. "And go through ten hours of labor."

Mack stared at his wife and then went behind her. "Come on, honey, you're almost done. One more push," he said encouraging her.

Jake looked stricken, his face was white and for a moment, Mack feared he was going to faint.

"Aargh," Anna cried. "It's coming."

"Push, Anna, push," she cried.

"Look, the head is crowning."

Jake looked down and Mack saw his legs crumple beneath him and the poor man landed on the floor.

With a laugh, Mack smiled at Anna. "Come on, our baby is arriving, push."

He could see she was giving it her all with her scream.

The cry of a baby suddenly filled the room and Mack all but jumped up to see if it was a boy or a girl. This was his child and he'd waited so long for this life to come into the world.

"A son," the midwife cried. "A baby boy."

Everyone in the room cried and was gazing at the crying boy.

"Well, his lungs are working fine," Anna said, gazing at the baby. "Give me my son. I want to hold him."

The midwife wiped his face and then handed the scissors to Mack. "Would you like to cut the cord?"

"Yes," he said as he took them from her hand and severed the ties between mother and child.

Then she wrapped his son in a blanket and handed him to Mack just as Jake begin to wake from his faint.

"Look, honey, he's staring at us," Mack said as he handed the infant to his wife.

Tears streamed down Anna's cheeks. "Welcome to the world, little one. Your other father is on the floor in a faint."

Jake stood and came to the other side of the bed. "Sorry. I was just so shocked to see you in so much pain. It got to me."

Anna reached up and stroked his cheek. "I survived and look at the son we created."

Mack and Jake glanced at one another and smiled. "Our first born."

"Thank you, Anna," Mack said and reached down and kissed her.

Jake grinned. "A boy."

Just then the baby started to squall, and Anna looked at them. "Somehow I think our life is about to change."

THANK you so much for reading Two Cowboys' Christmas Bride. I hope you enjoyed Jake, Mack and Anna's story. Please leave a review.

What's next? Look for Two Cowboys One Bride coming in February 11th.

TODAY WAS Belle Walker's wedding day. Uneasiness gripped her as she sat in the bridal room at the church waiting for the ceremony to begin. The chapel was filled with people from town and she had heard the whispers regarding her marriage.

No, she wasn't in love, but no other man had courted her. No one seemed to want her and she was nearing the old maid age of twenty-one. She wanted a home and family, children and a man to love and take care of her.

Was Lester Clark the man to give her what she wanted? Share his bed and bear his children?

A sigh escaped her as she thought of her own parents. An only child, they had left her wealthy and alone when they passed from this world to the next. She had a modest home in town, where she could comfortably live her life, but that wasn't what she wanted.

Sitting in the church, she stared out the window at the beautiful Texas sky. Living in Blessing, Texas there were not that many eligible men and if she didn't marry Lester, than who knew if she would ever have the chance to meet and marry another man.

She could be alone. The old man Walker or the crazy lady in town.

The sound of voices laughing and joking came to her and she realized it was Lester and his friend Randal Jones, his best man. They sounded drunk.

When she glanced out the window, she saw them staggering towards the church.

"Are you certain you want to do this," Randal asked. "She's short and chubby."

His words stung. No, she wasn't tall and her figure had often been described as voluptuous. But this monster was calling her fat.

"She's rich," Lester said with a grin. "She's wealthy

and after tonight, I will never have to crawl between her legs again. She thinks we're building a hotel together, but just as soon as I can, I'm headed to the gold fields of California. Or who knows she could suffer an accident."

Tears sprung in her eyes. Lester was willing to kill her in order to get to her inheritance?

"You dirty dog you," Randal said with a laugh. "Now I understand what you're doing. I don't know if I feel for her or think you're the smartest man I know. Marry the heiress and then end her life and live off the spoils."

Lester grinned and slapped Randal on the back. "This is why I've been drinking all morning. Look at what I'm marrying. Could you fuck that?"

A gasp escaped her at the coldness of her soon to be husband. She hung her head in shame. Was she that ugly?

How had she thought that marrying Lester would be right for her?

"Come on man, let's get in the church, so I can marry this little heifer," he said with a laugh.

Pain ripped through Bella as she stared around the room where brides had waited for years. What was she doing? Was she willing to settle for a man who obviously didn't love and planned on killing her?

"Oh, hell no," she said suddenly standing.

She had to get out of here. She had to get away now.

Peeking out the door, she glanced around the church and saw the back door. There was no way she was marrying Lester. Not now. Not ever.

Running out through the door, she lifted the skirts of her white silk wedding gown and ran down the streets.

The people walking cast her an odd glance as she ran to the stable where her stallion was kept.

She quickly saddled the horse and climbed on. She didn't have a clue where she was going, only that she had to escape the wedding.

She hiked her dress up around her legs, not caring that someone saw her chubby legs and kicked the horse.

"Let's go, Midnight. Time to get away. Time to escape."

The horse neighed as they raced out of the stable yard and through the streets of Blessing, Texas. A runaway bride who just needed to ride until she knew where she was going. Until she cleared her head of Lester and his lies.

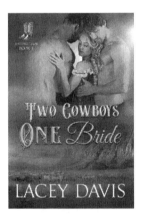

To Continue Reading the Next Adventure Click Here!

PLEASE LEAVE A REVIEW

Did you enjoy the book? Reviews help authors. I would appreciate you posting a review. Click here to leave a review.

Follow Lacey Davis on Facebook.

Sign up for my New Book Alert and receive a free book.

Also By Lacey Davis

Blessing, Texas Series
Loving My Cowboys
Two Cowboys' Christmas Bride
Two Cowboys One Bride
Two Cowboys Too Perfect
Two Cowboys to Protect Her
Two Cowboys Save Christmas

Bridgewater Brides World
Their Perfect Bride
Their Tempting Bride
Their Scandalous Bride—October 2021

Want to learn about my new releases before anyone else? Sign up for my New Book Alert and receive a complimentary book. Blindfold Me.

ABOUT THE AUTHOR

Lacey Davis is a pseudonym for a USA Today bestselling author who wanted to try her hand at writing sexy romance. With these novels, I hope to write sizzling romances that will leave you grabbing a fan to cool yourself off.

If you like hunky bad boy heroes who like to be in charge and strong pretty women who are willing to risk it all, then look no further. These sexy reads will get you in the mood. Come experience strong women who will tame these bad boys and leave them wanting more.

The End

Printed in Great Britain
by Amazon

69038409R00086